I0777652

Finding My Home

DARK REIGN SESSION 2

NATALIE ARTHUR

Copyright © 2023 by Natalie Arthur

Warning: All rights reserved. The unauthorized reproduction or distribution of this copyrighted work is illegal. Criminal copyright infringement, including infringement without monetary gain, is investigated by the FBI and is punishable by up to 5 years in federal prison and a fine of $250,000. This is a work of fiction.

Names, characters, places and occurrences are a product of the author's imagination. Any resemblance to actual persons, living or dead, places or occurrences, is purely coincidental.

Stealing is bad. Don't do it.

Cover Design by **Bookin' it Designs**

Formatting by **Natalie Arthur**

Finding My Home is part of the Dark Reign Session 2 Series, but it includes characters from my Mancini Legacy series and my Cimaruta MC Chicago Series. All my books are all stand alone with NO cheating and HEA.

Even though they are standalone, they are best enjoyed if read in order.

❀ Created with Vellum

Acknowledgments

Jessica, you are summer and I am winter. Always.

JD, thank you for spending late nights with and making sure I listened even when I didn't want to. Love you.

Kristen, we can do this. Together.

Nicole, I'm forever grateful that you're in my life.

Carissa, thank you for everything you do.

Danni, this journey is so crazy! Thank you for being here with me!

Tammy thank you for everything. For loving my books and supporting me.

Arthur, you've always supported me no matter how crazy my ideas are. I love you so much.

Mom, you've always been my biggest supporter and I don't know where I'd be without you.

Caoimhe-Lea, you drive me absolutely fucking crazy. But I wouldn't have it any other way. Love you.

Taye, Mary, Gretchen and everyone I'm forgetting who has supported my crazy ideas and continue to be with me, thank you. I truly couldn't do this without all of you.

Information

No part of this book or graphics were made
with AI.
HUMAN CREATION ONLY

Finding My Home has NO cheating and a
guaranteed HEA. It's part of the Dark Reign
Session 2 Series. And is connected to my Mancini
Legacy Series and my Cimaruta MC Chicago
Series.

Check out my website for current news and trigger
warnings.
Mancini Legacy and Cimaruta MC family trees.
Nataliearthurbooks.com

Mancini Legacy and Cimaruta MC Dictionary

Cage - Motorized vehicle with four wheels. (Cars)

Chicago Panthers - Professional baseball team.

Chicago Redhawks - Professional hockey team.

Cimaruta MC, Chicago - Chicago Motorcycle club, Mother charter

Cut - Vest that patched in members of the MC wear to identify who they are and their rank.

Lake Renegade Township - Town owned by the Mancini family.

Lucciola Island - 'Firefly' Island, owned by the Mancini family and located in Massachusetts.

Lucciola Memorial Hospital - Hospital in Lake Renegade Township.

Mancini Grill - 5-star restaurant located inside the Legacy Hotel.

Rockers - Top rocker has the club's name on it, the bottom rocker has the club's location.

Sprite Lake Village - Town in Illinois, owned by the Laurent family.

The Legacy Hotel - Hotel in downtown Chicago owned by the Mancini family.

Galway - Town in Ireland.

<u>ITALIAN</u>

Amore - Love.

Coglione - Asshole.

Colomba mia - My dove.

Cugino - Cousin.

Cuore mio - My heart.

Dolcezza - Sweetness.

Famiglia - Family.

Figlio - Son.

Fratello - Brother.

Fratellino - Baby brother.

Il mio mondo - My world.

Il mio pinguino - My penguin.

Mai Andato - Never Gone.

Mi dispiace - I'm sorry.

Mi passerotta - My little sparrow.

Nonno - Grandfather.

Nonna - Grandmother.

Ti abbiamo aspettato - We waited for you.

Ti voglio bene - I love you.

Zio - Uncle.

Zia - Aunt.

<u>IRISH</u>

Aintín - Aunty

Is í Gàidhlig ár gcéad teanga - Gaelic is our first language.

M'anam - My soul

Mo stór - My treasure.

<u>FRENCH</u>

D'accord petite sœur - Okay little sister

Je t'aime et Lorenzo - I love you and Lorenzo

Je t'aime - I love you

Je vous aime tous les deux - I love you both

Princesse - Princess

Toujours - Always

Toujours mes frères - Always my brothers

Tu es ma princesse - You are my princess

MANCINI FAMILY

Pietro & Alessia
Grandparents

Enea (T)
Son

Antonio (T)
Son

Leonardo (T)
Son

Gráinne
Daughter-in-law

Rosaura
Daughter-in-law

Sebastiano*
Grandson

Salvatore^
Grandson

Domenico*
Grandson

Fiorella^
Granddaughter

Lorenzo+
Grandson

Gianluca^
Grandson

Giovanna+
Granddaughter

Rowan
Great Grandson

(T) = Triplets
* = Twins
+ = Twins
^ = Triplets

FAUSTO & LUNA
GRANDPARENTS

GIACOMO
SON

CAITRÍONA
DAUGHTER IN LAW

CELESTINO
GRANDSON

FRANCESCO
GRANDSON

SAOIRSE
GREAT GRANDDAUGHTER

ISABELLA
GRANDDAUGHTER

LUCIANA
GRANDDAUGHTER

GRAYSON
GREAT GRANDSON

BASTIANINI
FAMILY

O'Connor
FAMILY

LIAM & RIOGHNACH
GRANDPARENTS

AIDEN
SON

GRÁINNE
DAUGHTER

ÉLODIE
DAUGHTER=IN LAW

ENEA
SON-IN-LAW

EMMERSON
ELIAS
EASTON *
EZRA *
EDEN
GRANDKIDS

SEBASTIANO *
DOMENICO *
LORENZO *
GIOVANNA *
GRANDKIDS

TWINS *

KEARNEY FAMILY

Liam & Orfhlaith
GRANDPARENTS

Caitríona
DAUGHTER

Giacomo
SON IN LAW

Celestino
GRANDSON

Francesco
GRANDSON

Saoirse
GREAT GRANDDAUGHTER

Isabella
GRANDDAUGHTER

Luciana
GRANDDAUGHTER

Grayson
GREAT GRANDSON

Cimaruta MC

President - Giacomo 'Forza' Bastianini

Vice President - Celestino 'Giustizia' Bastianini

Sgt-At-Arms - Francesco 'Bestia' Bastianini

Treasurer - Luciana 'Fuoco' Bastianini

Secretary - Isabella 'Dolce' Bastianini

Historian - Caitríona 'Forte' Bastianini

Road Captain - Connor 'Azrael' Byrne

Chaplain - Brennan 'Raziel' Doyle

Enforcer - Liam 'Amante' Murphy

Enforcer - Valentino 'Ombra' Marconi

Enforcer - Romana 'Fantasma' Vietti

Enforcer - Mitchell 'Granchio' Harris

Enforcer - Hollis 'Cavallo' Taylor

Enforcer - Rónán 'Ghiaccio' O'Callaghan

Enforcer - Fintan 'Toro' O'Callaghan

Prospect - Anthony Grimes

MANCINI FAMILY

- Antonio (T)
- Enea (T)
  - Gráinne
    - Sebastiano*
      - Schuyler
    - Sansone
    - Domenico*
    - Lorenzo+
    - Giovanna+
      - Declan
    - Rowan
- Leonardo (T)
  - Rosaura
    - Salvatore^
    - Fiorella^
    - Gianluca^

(T) = Triplets
* = Twins
+ = Twins
^ = Triplets

GIACOMO
CAITRÍONA
CELESTINO
ISABELLA
FRANCESCO
LUCIANA
MAEVE
RÓNÁN
SAOIRSE
GRAYSON
BASTIANINI
FAMILY

Athanasiou
(Polar Bear shifters)

Zeus & Athena

Ares
Eros
Adonis
Apollo
Artemis

*Ares, Eros and Adonis are triplets
**Apollo and Artemis are twins

NIKOLAIDIS
(WHITE TIGER SHIFTERS)

Panagiotis & Stella

Georgios

Kostas

Calliope

*TRIPLETS

Contents

Finding My Home

Chapter One

Niccolò

My last memory of my papà is him being shot—I was five years old.

My parents always made it a point for us to have dinner together. That night wasn't any different, except that we were out at my papà's favorite Italian restaurant. I remember laughing and having a good time. All of a sudden, a loud popping noise rang out and my papà fell to the ground. That was the day I learned about the Southside Mafia and how my Zio Elio was the boss. Zio Elio was someone who would come over for barbecues and parties, he even came to our sports events. My brothers and I played hockey and baseball when we were kids and he was part of our family.

When I was thirteen, I found out why my papà was killed. He was the consigliere for Elio, his right hand man. And when I turned sixteen, Zio Elio brought me into the organization. I started at the bottom and worked my way up to being his consigliere.

My sister, Stella, is the oldest of the five of us. We have three brothers between us, Armando, Carmelo and Marcello. We're all two years apart and extremely close. My sister is an accountant. She's the only one with a traditional job, the rest of us work with Elio. But she takes care of all the books for the Southside mafia and is in negotiations to take care of the Mancini and Cimaruta MC books too. She's seriously awesome.

The Southside Mafia has always been in business with the Mancini mafia. They're a mixed family that came here from Italy and Ireland a long time ago. Pietro Mancini and Liam Kearney came to America to give their children a different life and ended up creating a legacy for them. When Elio's papà, Vincenzo, formed the Southside mafia, he contacted Pietro and Liam. They figured out that working together would be beneficial for all of them, and they weren't wrong.

When Elio and the second generation of the Mancinis took over, they all decided to change the old ways. Try to make us legitimate business people instead of gangsters. Then, the Cimaruta MC became involved with all of us. Graínne Mancini, Enea's wife, and Caitríona Bastianini, the wife of Giacomo Bastianini, President of the Cimaruta MC, found each other again after losing touch back in Ireland. They're the reason we're all in business together, and now some of our guys are prospecting for the MC. Something I'm still considering.

A man like me doesn't get to have the normal family life. I learned that when I was a child and watched my papà be murdered. He was a good family man, yet he was gunned down, leaving behind a wife and five children. Not because of his family life, but because of who he chose to be outside of that life. My papà was the love of my mamma's life, but after he was taken from her, she was lucky enough to find love for a second time. When I was eight, she and Elio fell in love and he became our step-papà. Within four years, he and my mamma had three of their own babies, Alfonzo, Vincenza and Gervasio. We were all treated the same, and I think my papà would be happy for all of us. Even though my mamma was fortunate to find love a second time with Elio, I know she worries everyday that he could be taken away from her too. I don't want to do that to anyone. Especially not to any children that I would have if I chose a wife.

A few months ago, Elio made me his consigliere. That means I'm his second-in-command and his confidant. It's the position my papà had when he was killed. My mamma has been more worried about me since my promotion. But I told her that we're not the same organization that we were when my papà died. We've worked really hard at changing some of the ways we work. Not that we aren't in the grey areas still, but we're trying to do better. I'm not sure it's helps her fears.

In the last few years, I've gotten close to the Mancini and Bastianini kids. There are four in each of the other families, mine is the largest, including my half siblings.

Mirabelle

I don't remember my biological parents. My father shot my mother and then himself when I was two. They were on one of their drug benders and I guess my father just lost it. My sister Schuyler was seven and somehow even then, she was taking care of me. It's always been the two of us, Squirrel and Mouse. She calls me 'Mouse' because she said I didn't talk for a while after my father killed my mother. And when I did, it was like I was just squeaking at her. I was in the apartment when it happened, apparently he forgot I was there. Or that's the theory the police had because he didn't kill me too. My sister had been in school when it happened and she's always said that she was terrified when she got off the school bus and saw all the police cars and ambulances. She was so worried that they were there for me.

After our parents died, we spent the next eleven years in foster care. Our social worker, Miss Janice, made sure we were always placed together. She even made sure that any prospective parent knew that if they wanted one, they had to take both of us. We were a package deal that could not be split up, no matter what the reason was. So instead of being adopted, we moved from foster home to foster home. In the end we had a total of twelve.

We stayed with one family a little over a year, it was nice to be somewhere steady. That family was nice to us, but then it was time to move on. They talked about adopting us, but it never happened. There was only one other family I really liked, but we were only there for a few months.

When Schuyler was eighteen, she petitioned the court to get custody of me. And she applied to the Chicago Fire Department. All because of me. She didn't want me going to foster homes alone. So a few months before she aged out, Miss Janice helped her file all her paperwork for my guardianship and for her firefighter/EMT application. She made sure she had everything in order and deadlines were met, she even wrote her the best recommendation ever. When Schuyler turned eighteen, she had a job, an apartment and a thirteen year old kid.

Schuyler has worked her ass off making sure I never needed anything. Even when I was being an asshole to her, she never gave up on me. She always encouraged me to be the best that I could be. What I chose to be is a social worker like Miss Janice. I want to help other kids like Squirrel and me. Help keep siblings together and make sure they can survive after foster care. So many of them are left to figure out what to do on their own and that makes me sad. Because without Miss Janice, who knows where we would be today. My goal is to get my Doctor of Psychology degree and work with kids like us.

After Schuyler finished her training, she went to work at Station 5. That's where she met Captain Michael Jeffries, and he introduced us to his wife, Lynn. They became the parents we always wanted, the family we wished for growing up.

This year I turned eighteen and I'll be going to Blue University here in Chicago on a full scholarship. I've worked hard all through high school and on top of doing AP classes, I was able to take core classes at Blue University. So I won't be a typical 'freshman' when I start college. I already have my BS in Psychology. I'll be getting my Master's in Psychology and I should be able to finish that in two years and then off to my clinical studies for my Psy D degree. The only way I won't succeed is if I give up. And I can't do that, I owe it to my sister to be the best I can be and then take care of her.

Schuyler has been with Blaine Blackwell for a little over three years. I know he's hurting her, but I don't know why she won't leave him. She's always been the strong one and tells me all the time to never let a man rule my life. Never let a man mistreat me in any way or disrespect me. But that's what she's doing, letting that scumbag disrespect her and it's killing me. I hope that with me moving out and into the dorms, she will finally leave him.

Chapter Two

Niccolò

There's been some bad blood between the different families in Chicago. The Mancini family is the largest of all three, Southside is next and the Laurent family is the smallest. All of our territories touch each other and sometimes that means wars can happen. Never between us and the Mancinis. If that ever happens, it gets squashed pretty fast. But then there's the Laurents. Two decades ago, they kidnapped the youngest Mancini twins. Enea was told that they were dead. That should've started a war, but because Enea Mancini couldn't prove that it was them, he couldn't retaliate. Enea was the start of our different thinking. Elio tells me all the time that he would've started a full-out war if it had been him back then. But that now he understands why Enea didn't go after them. Starting wars is what we did in the old days. Proof? Fuck proof. If anyone slighted one of us, they died. Which is how I lost my papà. If things had been different then, maybe he would still be alive.

Even though we're trying to be better at how we deal with things, there are some things that just can't be overlooked. Enea told us that the reason Dorian Laurent is still alive, even after knowing he's the one who took his twins, is because his twins asked him to spare his life. When they were taken, they were raised as Laurents. They were loved and cared for, treated as if they were truly Laurents. Lorenzo and Giovanna asked Enea to spare Dorian's life. He did that for them. If they hadn't asked, there would be one less mafia boss in Chicago.

Ever since the twins were found and they made that request to their papà, there has been a truce between the three families. But now there's a new family trying to weasel their way into our territory. The Koslov family, who are originally out of Russia, now they have a base here in Aurora, Illinois, which is about an hour west of the city. But lately, they've been poking their noses around Chicago. And it's making everyone a little nervous. The Russians are not your typical mafia and they don't give a fuck that we're all trying to change. In fact they've told us that they'll never change, the old ways are the only way to do business. Fuck.

It's time for a council meeting. In the recent years, the council meetings are between all three families. The boss, their consigliere and sometimes the third-in-command.

"Any news on where the Russians are?" Elio asks everyone.

"Last chatter that Sebastiano heard was that they're trying to find a way into our areas. Seeing which of the three families are the weakest. They haven't figured out that we're working together yet," Enea responds.

"We heard the same thing. Rumors are that they're looking into the Cimaruta MC also," Elio says. "They want all of us gone."

"Maybe we need to bring the MC into our council meetings. They need to know what they're facing too."

Elio nods. "We should call them in and then resume this meeting."

Enea gets up and makes the call to Giacomo Bastianini, President of the Cimaruta MC,

Chicago chapter. After he hangs up, we wait for the MC council to show up. It takes them about twenty minutes and now we're all sitting for the meeting.

"We wanted to bring you in because the information we're hearing about the Russians is that they're not only coming after us, they're looking at you too," Elio says to Giacomo.

"We appreciate that, do we know what they want?" he asks.

"No. Right now all we know is that they're watching us and seeing what we do. I know that they want our territory, but I don't think they know that we're phasing out the gun running and drugs. I'm worried that they'll bring in more guns and drugs. Chicago can't afford more shit on the streets." Enea sighs.

Enea's right, in the last few years, we've been able to curb the amount of drugs and illegal guns that are on the streets. But if the Russians are going to start trying to sell their shit, it's going to be harder for us to control.

"So what do we do to keep them from selling in our territories?" I ask everyone.

"We should start with having a meeting. All of us should be there. Now if we do this, they'll know how our hierarchies work. Which I suppose really isn't a secret. But we'll have to be more on the lookout," Elio says. "Maybe it's time Southside gets the trackers put in."

The Mancinis and the Cimaruta have tracking devices implanted into them. I've seen first hand how that can help when someone goes missing.

"I'm not sure why we've waited, but I agree it's time," I add in.

"We can make that happen whenever you're all ready," Enea says.

Enea's oldest son, Sebastiano, developed the software for the chip and earlier this year we got to see it in action. The youngest daughter of the Cimaruta MC was kidnapped and thanks to her tracker, it was easier to find her.

"I can have him here within the hour if you're all ready," he says to us.

We all agree to do it now.

"Let's get lunch ordered and wait for Sebastiano," I say as I get online to order our lunches.

After a good lunch, we all got our trackers in,

testing them out to make sure they all work. I think we had more fun hiding to test it than we should've. It was a good day. But now we need to be ready to meet with the Russians. I can feel a battle coming on and I hope we all make it out unscathed.

"So I'll set the meeting up with Fyodor and let all of you know when and where it'll be. I think we'll be smart to have some of our guys around just in case," Elio says.

All the leaders agree that's the safest way for all of us. The one thing we've had to adjust to when working with the new factions is that the Cimaruta MC has women on their council. Giacomo's wife and their twin daughters are council members. In our world, women aren't usually in the inner circle. But Giacomo believes that his women are just as capable as his men. And I have to admire him for that. One day maybe we'll have women in high positions within the mafia.

Mirabelle

I can't wait to be out of high school. I don't have many friends here, they all look at me like I'm a

he started in on me last year. For some reason
st hates me and I have no idea why. But I do
st to just ignore the bitch. It's not just me she
er group picks on, and this school claims to
a 'no bullying' policy. But nothing ever
ens to her. So I stopped reporting it.

ucking loser!" Darcy yells to me.

wo. Months. I can do this. I walk past Darcy
her lemmings and I hear them laughing.
've never physically touched me, just mocked
ith their words. So I try to remember that
g 'sticks and stones.' But I wonder if whoever
that up got verbally bullied. It's not always
o say that words don't hurt. Because they sure
l do.

freak because of how much I study. They don't get
that I have to do this. Squirrel has always done for
me, I want to help her and do things for her too.
But I can't until I finish college. The one good thing
is that my hard work will pay off. I can basically
skip my first four years and graduate not only with
my high school diploma, but with my Bachelor of
Science too. Then I would start my freshman year
of college getting my Masters. I'm so excited for
that. To finally be somewhere that I can make a
difference. Part of my scholarship is that I get to
work in my field under Miss Janice.

Five more months, the countdown is on. And
the icing on all of this? I'm hoping Squirrel will
leave Blaine. She thinks I don't know what's going
on. I know he's hurting her, but I've never seen him
physically hurt her. The mental abuse is just as
bad. Some nights I hear her sobbing and I hate him
more and more. Thank god he doesn't live with us,
that's one thing she's never let him do. At the most,
he stays one or two nights, never more.

"MOUSE! You're gonna be late. Do you need
a ride to school?" Schuyler's voice booms through
my door.

I open the door and she knocks on my face. I
start laughing.

"Rude."

She hugs me. "I thought I heard you squeaking around up here. But I wasn't one hundred percent positive." She laughs.

"You're such a dork." I laugh. "But if you're offering a ride, I'm not going to say no."

Schuyler has an odd schedule, she works twenty-four hours then she's off for forty-eight. At the beginning when she started, it was harder because I was younger. When we met Cap and Lynn, they helped us out a lot. Mamma Lynn took me to school and picked me up when Schuyler worked. Then when I turned fifteen, we moved to an apartment that had a school bus stop. That definitely made it easier for Schuyler. Some days Mamma still picked me up and we got to hang out for the rest of the day.

"Five months. Can you believe it? Just five more months and I don't have to come here ever again," I say to Schuyler as we pull up to my school.

"I don't know if I tell you often enough, but I'm so damn proud of you. You're an incredible kid."

I blush at her comment. She tells me all the

time, making sure I know how and is proud of me.

"You know you say that t giggle.

"Well it's the truth. I don lucky to have you as my sist every day."

"You've always done for n saying I see you and what you give back to you."

"You don't have to give any Your happiness is my reward fc

I need to get out of the c me cry.

"Have a great day, do you n pick you up? I'm not doin laundry." She smiles at me.

I nod. "That would be awe see you after school."

"Still need your big siste school?" I hear one of the r sneering at me.

Chapter Three

<u>Six months later</u>

Niccolò

Two months ago, I took on another job. Bodyguard. I'm still consigliere for Elio, but I don't take care of any territories anymore. My brothers split up my area and are taking care of it together. Now I take care of Schuyler Mancini, she's the wife of Enea's oldest son, Sebastiano. All of the women in the Mancini, Bastianini and the Southside families have bodyguards. It's just part of our lives.

Last month, she was attacked by her abusive fuck of a boyfriend, Blaine Blackwell, who she was trying to leave. Then after we took care of Blaine, his father, Conrad, had her kidnapped. We learned that Conrad was part of the Russian mafia, he was the cousin of Fyodor Kozlov. He's the same fuck who's trying to take over our territories. And now he's pissed cause his cash cow is dead. Apparently Conrad had a lot of money, oh well. We couldn't leave them alive, you don't get to hurt women and live. Fuck that.

Now our problems with the Russians are worse. But there's nothing we can do to change that. All we can do is move forward and get rid of all of them.

There was one bright shining light in all that's happened. Mirabelle Viñales, Schuyler's younger sister. She's the most beautiful woman I've ever laid my eyes on. And she's so far out of my league that I don't know what to do. I should leave her alone, she's too good for the world I live in. But I can't let her go. She's in every thought I have, every dream I dream. And she feels the same about me. Me, the killer, the morally grey man who if given the choice, will kill anyone who hurts anyone I love—without hesitation or regret.

Mirabelle knows what I do for a living, and yet she still wants to be with me. I've never shared this part of my life with a woman, one night and that's the end. No need to get close and tell each other our secrets. But with Mira, it was already out there, I couldn't hide who I was. And she doesn't seem to mind what I do, even knowing I had a hand in what happened with Blaine and his father.

Elio and I have been talking about getting Mirabelle a bodyguard too. Not just because of how I feel about her, but because of what's happened to Schuyler.

"Have you decided on who to ask about being Mirabelle's bodyguard?" Elio asks me.

"I was thinking of asking one of my brothers. Carmelo was saying how he's wanting to do something different. I think he would do well to protect Mira."

"I trust your judgment. So whoever you choose, I'll back you. But if it's Carmelo or one of your other brothers, make sure they know that their territories have to be divided. I don't want them split between that and protecting Mirabelle."

"Agreed, I was planning on talking to them this weekend and see who wants to. They're the ones I trust the most with her."

Elio smiles and nods at me. "You boys are an important part of my organization. Even if each of you decide to be bodyguards instead of my capos, you're still important."

"Thank you. There are times I miss overseeing territories, but I have to admit taking care of Schuyler is very rewarding, and it keeps me on my toes. Or should I say she keeps me on my toes. Sebastiano has his hands full with her." I laugh.

"You're sure Mirabelle is the one you want?"

"She is. I know I was always saying no to relationships. But she's got me. I don't know how to walk away from her, even though I know it would be the smart thing to do. I just can't."

Elio chuckles. "I get it. When you meet that one, that's when you know what true love really is. I was always sad for your mamma when your papà was killed. I tried my best to stay on the side and just help all of you. But then one day..."

I make a face at him. "Ugh. I get it, I don't need the details."

Elio bursts out laughing. "Just know that I would never hurt your mamma. It's been sixteen years since the day I realized what I felt for her. She's my everything."

Hearing Elio say how much he loves my mamma makes me happy. I know that she'll always be taken care of no matter what. And I appreciate that from him.

A few hours later, my siblings and I are at our mamma's house. We're having a family dinner, plus I need to talk to them about who wants to take the job with Mirabelle.

"So it's really up to you three to decide who wants to be a bodyguard instead of being capos," I say to them.

"So if we want to be a bodyguard, we have to give up our territory?" Armando asks.

"That's right. I don't want your priorities split. Both jobs are important and I feel like if you're doing both, one will get less attention." Elio chimes in.

"So what happens to our territory? We split it like we did with Nico's?" Carmelo asks.

"Yes, the thing with being Mirabelle's bodyguard is that you'll have to move in with her. We arranged for her to move into an apartment. It has two bedrooms, two bathrooms and it's a five minute drive to the campus. It's different from Nico's situation with Sebastiano and Schuyler. Even if he lives with them, he doesn't have to be with her twenty-four seven."

"Well you won't be with her twenty-four seven either." I laugh. "Just when I can't be."

My brothers smile at me, they know how I feel about Mirabelle. And they know that I only trust them to help me take care of her.

"I'll do it," Marcello says.

"Thank you, fratello. This means a lot to me and to Schuyler, she's been more worried about Mira lately."

"Family. This is what we do."

Marcello's right, when we were called on to help the Mancinis, none of us thought twice about it. It's how we were raised and what we do.

"Now that business is done, let's eat!" Elio exclaims. We help Mamma bring out dinner and we all sit to enjoy our family time together.

Mirabelle

"You're going to need to get better about having a bodyguard with you," Schuyler says to me.

I pout at her. "But I don't even know who it'll be or if he'll be a creeper."

She laughs at me. "Do you really think Nico

would choose someone like that to watch over you?"

Niccolò Marini. That man has swept me off my feet and I've been floating on clouds since I met him two months ago. He says I'm too good for him and he worries about our age difference. But I'm eighteen years old and graduated last weekend. "Geez, just the mention of Nico and you light up like a Christmas tree," Squirrel teases me.

"Shut up." I laugh, knowing she's right.

Schuyler's right. Nico would never choose someone for me that he didn't trust. I wish he could be my bodyguard, and we did talk about it. But he explained that he's too close to me to be able to do that. He can't be objective when it comes to any threat to me, even the slighted altercation and he would overreact. I get that, it doesn't mean I still don't wish it.

"Nico said they're choosing a bodyguard for me tonight. And he'll move into the apartment with me this weekend."

"See that's an even bigger reason Nico will trust whoever he chooses to watch over you. That person will be living with you. He has to trust them."

I nod. "I know. I just wish it was Nico. Not that

I don't like that he guards you. I don't worry about you when he's with you. But...well...you know."

Schuyler chuckles and hugs me. "I know, Mouse. I know. So, what should we have for dinner?"

"We can make spaghetti," I suggest.

"Sounds good."

We like to make dinner together whenever Skye is off duty. Lately Sebastiano has been joining us, and it's nice having him around. He makes my sister smile more than I've ever seen her smile before. I'm pretty sure they're going to move in together after I move out.

"So how are things with Sebastiano?"

And there's that smile. I love it. "It's good. He's coming over later if that's okay, he wanted to join us for movie night."

"Of course it's okay. Nico said he would be here soon, he's at his mamma's having dinner with the whole family."

"It's cute how they still have family dinners," Schuyler says. "We need to promise that we will have dinner at least twice a month. Maybe even once a week after you move out."

I put my pinky out for her. "Pinky promise."

After dinner, Nico and Sebastiano show up at the same time. We can hear them talking and Sebastiano is telling Nico that he better be serious and good to me. In the short time he's been with Schuyler, he's been a great big brother to me. And it makes me glad I'm not dating college boys. They'd run at the sight of the Mancini boys and the guys in the Cimaruta MC. I'll never admit it to them, but I love it. Before, it was just Squirrel and me, and now we have a big family.

I open the door before they can knock and the look on both their faces has me in stitches. Mid-sentence, mouths open. I hear Skye giggling behind me and turn to see her taking a picture of them.

Sebastiano charges in, scoops her up and kisses her.

"That better stay in your phone." He laughs.

"Oh hell no. This is going to everyone in the family." She squeals as he smacks her ass.

"Okay. That's not something I needed to see today." I laugh.

Nico comes in and kisses my cheek.

"You look beautiful," he whispers. His breath

on my neck sends shivers down my body. We haven't kissed yet, I can feel him holding back a little. I think it's because he's worried about hurting me, at least that's what he's told me. I just want to feel his lips on mine. Soon.

We hear someone clear their throat, I look up and see Marcello.

"Hi." I smile at him as I give him a hug.

"Hey, Mouse." He smiles back then goes to give Schuyler a hug too.

"So since you're here too, I'm guessing you're my new roommate?" I say to Marcello.

Marcello laughs and fist bumps me. "Roomie."

"You need to be careful, Marcello is the messiest of all of us. He has an aversion to using laundry baskets," Nico teases.

"It's okay, he has his own bedroom and bathroom. As long as it doesn't dribble out of his area, we're all good." I wink at Marcello.

"Hey! I'm not messy. In fact, Nico is the messy one. He's the baby and Mamma always did everything for him. Did you know she still does his laundry?" He snickers at Nico who punches him in the arm. "See? That's proof I'm not lying."

I laugh at the two of them. They remind me of Squirrel and me. Always picking on each other, but you can see and feel their love.

"So since it's Friday, you don't have school till Monday right? I'll need your school schedule too. And we're moving in this weekend," Marcello says taking a big breath after.

We all laugh at him. He's going to be fun to live with.

Moving into the apartment went smoothly and only took one day. Everyone came to help and they even gave us gifts of furniture. So there was nothing we had to buy. I don't know how to thank any of them enough.

I love this apartment, it's more than I'd ever be able to afford. And I feel safe here. Not only with Marcello staying here with me, but we're in a secure building owned by the collective that includes the Mancinis, Cimaruta MC and the Southside Mafia. Our apartment overlooks the Chicago river and Navy Pier. And at night you can see the lights from the ferris wheel. It also has the perfect view of Lake Michigan where they set off the fireworks.

Marcello has gone out tonight, there are things

he needs to finish up with his territories before Monday comes.

"How do you like the apartment?" Nico asks me as he wraps his arms around me from behind.

"It's perfect," I say softly as I lean back into him and we look out at the lake. "Thank you so much for helping me do all of this."

"I will do anything I can to make you safe," he says as turns me in his arms to face him. "Are you sure about us?"

"Yes," is all I say before he takes my mouth with his.

He uses his tongue to part my lips as I moan. I nip his lower lip as our tongues start to duel. His kiss is making my whole body tingle.

When we finally break apart, we're both panting.

"You taste like cotton candy," he whispers. "And I love cotton candy."

Nico leads me to the couch so we can snuggle and watch TV.

The next thing I know it's morning and I'm

lying on Nico. I wiggle around a tiny bit and hear him groan.

"Don't do that," he growls. My new favorite sound is his raspy morning voice.

I smile and look up at him, giving him my best innocent face. He chuckles at me and we fall asleep for a few more hours.

Chapter Four

I'm not sure how I kept myself from ravaging Mira last night. And then this morning when she was wiggling herself on me? She's such a minx, she knew what she was doing. I'm trying to be a gentleman, but she's not making it easy. I need her to be sure about us, she says she is but does she really understand what I do? I don't want to walk away from her, but if it's the only way to keep her safe, I will. And if she really is sure? Once I make her mine, there's no turning back for me. Somehow I knew this the day I met her.

"Hey Elio," I say when my phone rings.

"Need you home now. Marcello is almost there to stay with Mirabelle. And Sebastiano's with Schuyler," Elio says.

"Okay, I'll leave as soon as Marcello gets here."

I know better than to ask questions when Elio calls on me. And this time he sounds concerned. Knowing that he's already made sure Mira and Skye are okay makes me nervous.

"You have to leave?" Mira asks as she sits up.

"I do, I'm sorry. I was hoping to be able to spend all day with you. But I'll come back as soon as I can if you want."

She burrows herself into my chest. "Of course I want you to come back."

I kiss her head and sigh. Maybe I'm not a complete monster, I did something to deserve my little Squeak. Then again, who am I kidding?

We hear a key in the door and Marcello walks in. I kiss Mira as I'm getting up.

"Listen to Marcello. Whatever he tells you to do? You do it."

"Okay," she says softy as she hugs me. "Please be safe. I need you."

I hug her tight then go over to my brother.

"Do you know anything?" I ask him quietly.

"Just that it has to do with the Russians."

"Fuck. Okay."

"Don't worry, fratellino. I got your girl."

I sigh and nod. "I know you do, that's not what I'm worried about. I just hate leaving her."

Marcello chuckles. "Never thought I'd see the day when my fratellino would be in love with a woman. But it's a good look on you."

I punch him in the arm and laugh. "Text you later."

During the last gathering, Elio was supposed to make a call to Fyodor and set up a meeting. By the sound of his voice, that didn't go well. And that means my weekend is over. Fucking asshole Fyodor.

When I get to Elio's office, everyone is here waiting.

"Sorry it took me so long. I wanted to make sure Marcello got to the apartment before I left."

"Not to worry, we just got here too," Enea says.

"Well, I'll get right down to it. Fyodor doesn't want to meet with us, he doesn't want any part of what we stand for." Elio sighs. "This is going to cause a war, and knowing Fyodor, there's going to be casualties. I want my men on alert at all times. I don't want excuses. Nico, you work it out with Sebastiano and Marcello when it comes to protecting Schuyler and Mirabelle. It might even be a good idea for all of you to stay in the same home for now."

"Okay, I think that's a good idea too. But the apartment is too small for all of us, and Sebastiano shares his house with Domenico," I say.

"There's enough room in their house for all of you," Enea says. "Giovanna and Declan live on one side of them, and Fiorella and Cillian on the other side of Giovanna. If we need to close ranks more, we can all stay on our property. Between us and the Cimaruta, we can close off a huge area for everyone. And protect it."

"Maybe that's what we should do anyway. Is there enough room for our families?" Elio asks.

"Yes, there's enough room for all of your crew

and their families. I'll call Sebastiano and let him know to get things set up."

"And I'll call my boys and get them rounding up our families that don't live on the property," Giacomo says.

They both get up and make their phone calls.

"Do you think we really need to do all of this?" I ask Elio.

"I rather be over cautious than under. I don't trust Fyodor or his crew, and I wouldn't put it past them to come after anyone left outside. I will get your mamma and siblings to the property."

"Okay, I'll head back to the apartment and get Mirabelle and Marcello packed and we'll meet you there. How long should we plan for?"

"I don't know. That's going to depend on how long Fyodor wants to be an asshole."

I sigh. All this shit because the Russian mob boss wants to be a big fucking baby. I can't wait for this to be over so I can claim my girl.

Mirabelle

Watching Nico leaves sucks. I know whatever

the phone call was about is important, but it doesn't mean I have to like it.

"I'll print out my schedule for you and a map of the university," I say to Marcello.

"Thanks, it'll give me time to map out where you go. I know this isn't easy, but this isn't the normal way we live. It will get better."

I sigh. "I know, and I'll get used to it. I had a hard time in high school and well, college isn't as fun as I thought it would be. I'm in classes with people older than me. When they find out how old I am, they make comments about how I got into my master's program so early."

"Fuck 'em. You hold your head high and do what you do. Don't ever let anyone tear you down. And if they cause more problems? You point them out to me or Nico. No one will hurt you. I promise you that."

"Thank you, I really do appreciate you stepping in to be my bodyguard. Nico and I talked about him doing it, but I understand why he can't."

Marcello nods. "There's no way I could watch a woman that was as important to me as you are to him. I would lose focus anytime someone came near her."

"Nico growls at other guys." I giggle.

"You should know something about my baby

brother. He's never wanted a relationship with a woman before. I don't know why. He's dated, but I've never seen him look at someone the way he looks at you. So I'm asking you, if you aren't sure about him, or you need time to figure things out, let him know now. Please."

I look at Marcello, "I want to be with your brother. I don't know what it is, I can't explain it. But it's like he's that part of me that was missing. I felt it, but I never knew what that missing part was. Now I know it was him. He was missing."

Marcello grabs me in a bear hug. "Thank you."

I giggle as he squeezes me.

"Cant...breathe..."

He puts me down. "You're good for Niccolò. You bring light into his darkness and he needs it. Just remember that on his darkest days. Because he will have them. And those days you'll have to help him."

I'm not exactly sure what Marcello is talking about. But I know that no matter what, I'll be here for Niccolò.

"You don't need to worry."

I understand why he's worried, I worry about Schuyler the same way. It's less now because I know Sebastiano won't hurt her, but after what Blaine did to her...

I hear Marcello on the phone and he sounds concerned.

"Is everything okay?" I ask him.

"It will be. I need you to grab things you'll need for the next couple of weeks. And all your school stuff cause we won't be back here for a bit."

I frown at him. "Where are we going?"

"Staying at the Mancini property. They've decided it's safer for everyone to be there. And they have a huge property that we can be safe in."

"Will my sister be there too?"

"I believe so, I think everyone that's close to any of the Mancinis, Cimaruta MC and Southside will be there."

I nod and head to my room to pack a few bags. I'm a little sad, I mean we just moved into the apartment. I wonder what could be so bad that we have to be under lockdown. While I'm packing, Nico comes back to the apartment and I can hear him talking to Marcello. I can't hear what they're saying, I wish I could.

I feel Nico's arms circling my waist and he kisses my neck. Even if I can't see him, I always know it's him.

"Hi, handsome."

"Hi, my Squeak. Do you need me to do anything?"

I giggle at his nickname for me. The first time he called me that, I asked him why. He said Schuyler calls me 'Mouse' all the time. He wanted to keep in sync with a mouse, and well, they squeak. He's so funny.

"I'm okay, I just don't know what to take with me."

"If you need something, I'll bring you back to grab it. Don't stress on it."

I wish I could say I'm not worried, but I am. I'm worried not only for me, but for everyone. I hope whatever is going on, we all make it out okay.

Chapter Five

Niccolò

It takes a few days, but we finally get everyone settled at the property. The Mancini property is connected to the Cimaruta property. The third piece of land that connects to the Mancini and Cimaruta property is owned by two families that moved over from Greece earlier this year, the Nikolaidis and Athanasiou families. In the middle of the properties there's a campground where you can hike and fish and enjoy time on one of the many lakes. It's separated from the areas the families live and the security is tight. Right now, they've closed all the recreational areas and the cabins. They'll keep it all closed up until our business with the Russians is over.

It's relaxing being here on the property, we have about a month before it's too cold to swim in the lakes that are scattered on the property. We've been getting to know the two Greek families. There's something different about them, I can't quite put my finger on it. But they're good people.

I spot Mirabelle talking with her sister, they're laughing and playing in the lake. I love the smile that Mira has when she's really happy, she also has this fake smile that's hilarious.

Even though the atmosphere here is relaxing and almost tranquil, my intuition is telling me that something is going to happen. There's no way Fyodor has stopped coming after us.

"A penny for your thoughts?" I hear my Squeak say as she wraps her arms around me.

I smile and kiss her head, holding her tight.

"Just taking in how beautiful it is on the property," I lie to her. I don't want her to worry any more than she already is.

"I know you're lying, Niccolò." She looks up at me, frowning.

My girl. In the short time we've been together, somehow she's learned some of my quirks. I'm not sure that's a good thing, knowing what I do.

I chuckle, "I was wondering when things will change, because they will change."

"You mean the situation that's brought all of us here?"

I nod. "I don't think I could survive if something happened to you. You need to promise me that you will stick to Marcello if anything happens. I can't do my job if I'm worried about where you are. And Marcello's job is to protect you."

"I promise, Nico. You don't have to worry about me. If anything happens I will find Marcello."

I lean down and kiss her, I'm relieved to know that she understands what needs to happen. And I also know she wants to know more. But Schuyler has told me she's talked to Mira and explained that girlfriends don't usually get to know inside information. That changes when you become a wife. Girlfriend. Huh. I have a girlfriend, and I officially sound like a sap. Even if it's only in my head.

"Enea wants all council members to join in the meeting in fifteen minutes," my oldest brother Armando comes over to tell me.

"Thanks, I'll be there in a minute," I say to him, then turn to Mira. "You stay with Schuyler and the other women. I'm pretty sure Marcello needs to be at this meeting too. But don't worry, we will be right in that building over there."

"Okay. I really hope we can go home soon. I hate all this tension that I feel from everyone."

"Me too, Squeak. Me too."

When I join the meeting, we're still waiting for a few guys. But something's happened and it's not good. As soon as everyone is here, Enea stands up.

"I appreciate all of you coming to this meeting. There's a few things that have happened in the past few days. We weren't paying close enough attention because we were all trying to get here and settled. First, one of the Cimaruta prospects was attacked and he's fighting for his life right now. I'm going to let Giacomo tell you about him first."

"Thanks, Enea. Most of you know Anthony Grimes, he's been prospecting for us for the last year. He was gathering his family and was gunned down at his home. Thankfully his family's okay and they're here. So if we can all give them some extra support, that would be really great. His wife,

Trisha, is at the hospital as much as she can. But they have two little ones, so it's going to be hard. And the doctors don't know if he's going to make it."

"Was it Fyodor?" Carmelo asks.

"We think it was. There's no one else coming after any of us right now," Giacomo answers.

Everyone starts to get loud.

"Okay, we know what Fyodor and his crew want. We need to be smarter when we go out, and always watch our surroundings," Enea tells everyone.

"You said there was more?" Armando asks.

Enea nods. "This one, Elio needs to tell everyone about."

When Enea says that, a ball of dread starts to form in my belly.

"Thanks, Enea." Elio clears his voice and you can see him fighting back his emotions. He looks at my brothers and me. "Our house was burned down this morning."

"Holy fuck, what?" Carmelo yells.

"Eveyone's okay, we were already here. But Captain Michael Jeffries, Schuyler's fire captain, called her to tell her they were called to the house. They saved as much as they could, but most of it's gone."

"Fuck. So now we have to worry about our homes? Why can't we just take this assfuck and his crew out?" Sebastiano snaps.

"We will. We need a plan. I don't want to lose any more people. War is ugly and people will die, but if we play it smart, we can make sure most of us survive," Elio says.

We've been up against the Russians before. That one didn't work out so well for my family, and I don't think my mamma could take losing another member of our family.

Mirabelle

Something happened and it's not good. I watched all the big guys make their way to the meeting. Schuyler comes over to me.

"I need to tell you something. I've gotten permission to tell you, and it's something that Niccolò and his brothers are learning about right now."

I feel sick as she's telling me this. I don't know where his mom or his younger siblings are.

"D-did someone get hurt?" I whisper to her.

She shakes her head. "No, no one got hurt. But

their house was burned down this morning. Papa called me cause they got called to the fire."

I can't stop the tears that are falling. My poor Niccolò. He loved that house, it's the house they grew up in. And now it's gone? Schuyler wraps her arms around me.

"Everyone's okay? His mamma and brothers and sisters?"

"They're all okay, they were here when it happened."

That's a relief, but now this war is escalating. I don't understand why Fyodor needs to hurt people he doesn't even know. I pray that my family is intact after all of this is done.

"I know that Nico can't tell me things right now. But I'm scared. What if I'm at school and something happens to him? Or to you? I couldn't live if that happened."

"Mouse, you need to know that you're strong. You survived more than most people have. Even if you don't remember. You survived our parents, foster care, and now? You're one of the youngest people to get accepted into the Master's program at Blue University. You can get through anything."

I hold my sister tight. It's always been the two of us. I need it to be us when it's all over. We go over to Nico's mamma..

"I'm so sorry about your home," I say as I hug her.

"Thank you, sweetheart. The thing I'm grateful for is that my family is okay. But my Niccolò will need you. That was the last connection my older children had to their papà. They're going to have to deal with that and the situation that's going on."

"I got Niccolò's back one hundred percent."

His mamma hugs me tight. "I'm glad my Niccolò found you."

Hearing her say this makes my heart so happy. Having Nico's mamma's approval is very important. We see all the guys come out of the meeting. The Marini men look so somber, it makes me sad all over again. The worst part is that none of them really have time to grieve for what they've lost right now. They need to get this situation under control first.

When Blaine tried to kill my sister, he disappeared. We don't talk about it, but I know everyone here knows or had a part in it. Then Blaine's father Conrad disappeared and again, all I heard was bits and pieces. From what I do know? Fyodor is going to be taken care of too. I have no doubt. But I still have worries about who will be hurt in the process.

Chapter Six

Niccolò

It's taken us a week to figure out how and where we'll be staging things for Fyodor to finally come out of hiding. That cowardly bastard has been in hiding since he ordered the attack on Anthony and our home. Anthony is still in a coma and we don't know how he'll be if or when he wakes up. But he and his family have the full support of everyone here.

"You all know what part you'll be playing in the coming days. The Cimaruta will be here on the property taking care of everyone that's staying here.

But the rest of us will get back to our 'normal' routine. We need Fyodor and his crew to think we've gone back to normal. I think that's the only way he'll come out of hiding," Elio says to everyone.

"We know that you're all worried about your loved ones. But there are some of them that need to go back to work and school. All the little ones will be homeschooled for now. But the high school and college kids need to get back. Every one of them will have a bodyguard," Enea adds.

"I can't guarantee no one will be hurt when this is all over. I wish I could. But I can promise that we will take Fyodor and his crew out once and for all," Elio says.

The way Elio says that we're going to take care of Fyodor 'once and for all' makes me wonder what he means. It doesn't feel like it's just about what's going on now. I think I finally know why I've had this dreadful feeling for so long. Now I need to ask Elio if I'm right.

We go over our plans again, making sure no one is left without a bodyguard. And that all of us are never alone when we're out. Even though we're all trained in self-defense, there's no reason for us to take chances.

When the meeting's over, I head over to Elio.

"Can I talk to you for a second?" I ask him.

"Of course, what's up?"

"You said we're going to take out Fyodor 'once and for all.' Which tells me this isn't the first time we've had issues with him."

Elio's face changes as he realizes what I'm asking him.

"Did Fyodor or one of his men kill my papà?"

Elio takes a deep breath and sighs. "I knew one day we would have this conversation."

"Did he?" I frown.

"Yes. Fyodor was the one who pulled the trigger. It was his initiation into the mob. At the time I didn't know it was him. Your mamma couldn't identify him, none of you could. You all said the men that came in were wearing masks."

"So how do you know it was him?"

"He admitted it when I called him for the sit down. He said that he would finish off what he started nineteen years ago—"

"And nineteen years ago, Papà was murdered," I finish for him. "I want to be the one to end Fyodor. Promise me."

"You know I can't promise you that, Niccolò."

"Yes you can. I've never asked you for anything. I need this."

Elio stops and looks at me. "Okay, Niccolò. You will be the one to end this."

"Thank you," I say as he embraces me.

"For your papà. I miss him too."

I have no doubt that Elio misses my papà. They were best friends since they were kids, but he wasn't there when he died. We were and every one of us remembers it like it was yesterday. My nightmares are littered with my papà's face as he took his last breath. I need to finish this for all of us. To avenge my papà.

Mirabelle

Today I go back to school, out in the open after being on lockdown for the past two weeks. And I have to admit to myself that I'm terrified. I'll have Marcello with me, but I keep worrying about Schuyler. I can't go through what we did when she was taken, and I know that she's not really a target this time. That doesn't take away my fear.

"Are you ok, baby?" Nico asks as he wraps his arms around me. He's been staying with me since we've been at the Mancini property. I've been trying to figure out a way to ask him if he will move in with me.

"I'm okay, just a little nervous about going back to school."

"You can take more time off, you don't have to go back today."

I shake my head. "I have to go back, I have work to turn in and I don't want to miss more lectures."

"Marcello will be with you. And I'll come down whenever Sebastiano is with Schuyler. We have decided that we need to stay in the same house together. So we'll all be staying at Sebastiano and Domenico's house in Evanston. It's closer to your school and Schuyler's work."

I turn in his arms to face him. "Okay. I was hoping that you would be staying with me still. I've gotten spoiled these last two weeks. Going to bed with you and waking up with you, it starts my day off in the best way."

Niccolò leans down and kisses me, I moan softly as I nip his lower lip. He growls softly, it's a sound that never fails to make me wet for him. And I'm pretty sure he knows it. I run my hands down his back and down to his ass. He pushes me against the wall and rubs himself on me. Fuck, I need him.

"Please," I moan. "I need you, Nico."

"Are you sure? Once we cross this line, there is no going back."

I unbuckle his belt and open the buttons on his jeans.

"I've never been more sure of anything before," I say as I drop to my knees, taking his jeans down with me. He takes this moment to take his shirt off. Fuck, he's gorgeous, I'm pretty sure his muscles have muscles and the tattoos that cover his body? Fuck. I palm his cock through his boxers and he takes a sharp breath.

"Fuck," he gasps.

I pull his boxers down and take a moment to look at his cock. It's fucking glorious, I lick the precum off the tip. Then wrap my lips around the tip of his cock.

"Oh god, Mira. Just like that, baby."

I start to pump him with my hand as I take as much of him into my mouth as I can. Suddenly, he pulls me off him and carries me to our room. He gets my clothes off in record time and is grinning at me from between my legs. I watch him as he slowly licks me, I grab his head as I moan.

Niccolò

The sounds that are coming from my Squeak is making my cock dribble more and more precum. I suck her clit into my mouth as I slide a finger in her, slowly pumping it in and out. I add one more finger as I feel her getting close.

"Fuck yes, baby," she gasps as she comes.

I line myself up with her slit, I can't wait any longer to feel her wrapped around my cock. I slowly push into her.

"Fuck, you're so damn tight, baby."

I reposition her legs so I can slide in easier. I take a minute to let her adjust to me. She grabs my ass and makes me move. Her pussy is squeezing me like a vice and it's driving me crazy. I start to push in and out faster as I reach between us and pinch her clit.

"I need to feel you come all over my cock," I whisper.

She nods as I move faster.

"I'm gonna come, Nico," she moans.

"Fuck, yes. Come for me, baby."

I thought she was squeezing me before, but holy fuck the sensations as she's coming on my cock is fucking incredible. She's milking my cock as I follow her over the edge.

I hold her tight to me as we catch our breath.

"You're incredible, Mirabelle. I'm yours forever," I say softly as I kiss her.

"And I'm yours Niccolò. Always."

We fall asleep in each others arms, there's no better place to be.

Chapter Seven

Niccolò

After making love to Mira, I had a slight panic attack. I've never forgotten to use a condom, not once. But fuck me, I didn't even think about it. Although Mira being pregnant doesn't scare me in the least. I just don't want her to give up her dreams because I was an idiot and couldn't remember to wrap up. She assured me it was okay, she's on the pill. After hearing that, I was kind of sad. Yeah I know, I'm a dumbass. I want it both ways.

In two days, we go back to our 'normal' life. Well as normal as possible. My mamma and younger siblings will stay on the Mancini property. My youngest brother and sister are still in high school, but my mamma got permission to homeschool them for a while. In fact, all of the school-age kids have gotten permission to stay home. Only the ones in college are going, that includes my brother Alfonzo. He just started college this year, Armando will be his bodyguard for now. He's also at the same college as Mira so if there's any problems, my brothers will have each other until backup gets there.

Tonight we're having a barbecue, it's nice to have a night to relax. To not have to worry about what's going on outside the security walls. Because tomorrow, we will see Fyodor's next move.

"We should head to the house tomorrow. That way we can get settled and get ready for what's coming," Sebastiano says to us.

"Sounds good. And you're sure it's okay for all of us to stay there?" Carmelo asks.

"Definitely. And it's safer. We own three homes in a row, ours, Giovanna and Declan's and Fiorella and Cillian's. We can spread out between the three houses. And one cool thing? All three homes are connected through the basements. There's a tunnel to connect them." Domenico smiles.

"That's definitely cool. And that's a great way to keep everyone safer. Your sister and cousin both have guards?" Carmelo asks.

"Yes. Gia's bodyguard is Grady and Fiorella's is Marco. And they live with them too," Sebastiano answers.

Sometimes it's hard to know which twin is talking to me. Sebastiano and Domenico are identical twins. Most of the time I tell them apart because Schuyler is with Sebastiano. But I've been wrong before, and I told them that one day I'm gonna stick post-its on them.

Since going into business with the Mancinis and meeting the Cimaruta MC, things have changed. We always believed in family first, but the Cimaruta take it one step further. Making sure that they spend time together no matter how busy they are. The MC has a barbecue with their clubs once a month. It's to make sure the chapter clubs are following the rules. And to see if there's anything that the MC needs to take care of. They really are a family, and now they've welcomed us into it too.

As a family, we try to have dinner at Mamma's at least once a month. But for some reason, there's always one of us that can't make it. I think we need to change that. Mamma has been making comments about how she's not getting any younger...and grandbabies would be nice. Maybe Mira will help me give her that one day.

I see Elio gesturing for me to come over to him. "Enea and Giacomo want to have a quick meeting with us."

"Do you know what it's about?"

He shakes his head 'no' as we walk into the MC clubhouse.

"Thanks joining us in this meeting. There's a few things we felt we should tell the Southside guys about. But we had to get permission before we did anything," Enea says.

"So first of all, when I found this out, I didn't believe it. It's something out of folklore and well, I told Zeus that he was full of shit. But then he showed me what they were and holy fuck." Giacomo laughs.

Now I'm more curious than when we got in the room. What the fuck are they talking about? Folklore and showing what they are? Are they fucking monsters?

"I know you all know me and my family, what you don't know is that we're shifters," Zeus says.

"Grifters?" Carmelo asks.

Zeus laughs. "No. Shifters. We shift into animals."

The Southside guys start mumbling.

"See? I did the same thing, it sounds like bullshit, right? Fucking shifters. That's fantasy shit." Giacomo laughs more.

"There's no way you shift into animals." Marcello frowns.

"Let's go out back and we'll show you," Zeus says.

We all follow out to the private backyard of the clubhouse. It's a separate area from where the barbecue is being held.

"Now you need to know that this doesn't go beyond the people here. We can't let this knowledge get out, our species depends on secrecy. Panagiotis and I have gotten permission from our elders back in Greece to let you in," Zeus explains to us.

We all agree that whatever is shown to us will never be talked about outside of who's here. Which I feel is a given, because we never speak to anyone about what goes on in our meetings.

"Just know that in our animal forms, we're still ourselves. We think like we do now, we're just fuzzy. Now we aren't ashamed of getting naked in front of any of you. But we talked it over and decided that for this time, we'll shift and come out. It's less of a shock if you don't see the process."

I watch both families go behind a make-shift curtain that's off to the side. I still can't wrap my mind around the fact that they'll be animals.

"Holy fuck!" Carmelo gasps as we see the first of the shifters. It's a huge polar bear and it's stretching. Whoever that is has to stand almost seven feet tall.

"How do we know who it is?" Marcello whispers to Enea.

Enea chuckles. "I don't know. I can't tell you who is who. Except that those two that are huddled together? That's Kostas and Artemis."

We look to over to where a white tiger and a polar bear are nuzzling each other. Watching all the shifters walking around and coming up to us is crazy. One is nudging my arm and it sounds like it's laughing. What the fuck? It is soft...

After an hour of mingling, they go back and shift again. When they all come out, they're all smiles, I'm sure the looks on our faces are what's making them laugh.

"That was fucking incredible," I say to Zeus.

Zeus gives me a huge smile. "Thank you."

Suddenly I'm feeling a whole lot better about the coming war. Not only do I trust everyone here, we have shifters. Fucking polar bear and tiger shifters.

Mirabelle

I always love the Cimaruta barbecues. It's given me an even bigger family than I could've ever dreamt of. Next weekend Sebastiano and Schuyler are getting married. And she's expecting. I'm so excited to be an aunty, and the glow on my sister is incredible. I've never seen her so happy.

"Hey, Mouse. How are you doing?" Schuyler asks as she comes to stand next to me.

"I'm okay. How is my niece or nephew?" I ask as I rub her tiny bump.

"Baby is good. Who knew something the size of a peanut could make you so sick?" She laughs.

"Are you still feeling sick all day?"

"Not all day, but at least a few times a day. Doctor said that it's okay and it should get better."

I hug her tight. "I hope you feel better soon. I love you."

"It's all worth it for our peanut." She smiles as she rubs her belly.

Of course, Sebastiano is making a beeline for us. I'm not sure they know how to be apart anymore. I used to be a little jealous of the way Sebastiano looked at Schuyler. I wanted someone to look at me like that. And now? I have Nico, he looks at me like I'm the only woman he's ever looked at.

I look around for Nico and see him talking with Marcello. I know he's worried too, but Marcello won't be alone. I got to look at his brother Alfonzo's schedule and his classes aren't too far from mine.

I feel Nico's arms circle around me. I love the feel of him wrapping me in his arms. It makes me feel safe and secure. It's where I know I'm supposed to be. With Nico.

"Is everything okay?" I ask him.

"Yeah, everything is okay."

Even though I'm still worried about being back in school, I trust Nico and Marcello. I know they'd never let anything happen to me.

"Please be safe when you're with Squirrel, I need you both in my life forever," I say softly to him.

"You can't get rid of me that easily, Squeak," he responds as he turns me in his arms.

I look up at him and I can see how much he cares for me. I get on my tiptoes and kiss him. I think I'm falling in love with my mafia man.

Chapter Eight

Niccolò

Waking up with Mira in my arms is the best way to start my day. I get up and grab a quick shower, trying not to make too much noise. By the time I'm out and getting dressed, she's making grumbly noises. Schuyler has to be at the firehouse by four am, so we have to leave soon.

"I'm sorry, love. But I have to get going, text me when you're heading to school," I say softly to her.

Mira opens one eye and squints at me.

"Okay," she mumbles.

I chuckle and kiss her. "Please don't take any

unnecessary chances. No matter what. Promise me, Squeak."

"I promise." She yawns. "You better follow that rule too."

"I will," I say as I kiss her one more time and head to the kitchen to wait for Schuyler.

As I head to the kitchen, I smell fresh brewed coffee. We were ambushed at the Star Coffee that Schuyler always went to. Since then, he's been making her coffee each work morning so that she doesn't have to stop for it. Once in a while we do a drive-through, but never on a set schedule.

"Morning," I say to Sebastiano as I take the cup of coffee he just poured.

"Thief." He laughs as he pours himself another cup.

"You going back to the office today too?"

"Yeah, I need to get shit done and it has to be done there. It feels weird to be acting like everything's 'normal.'" He sighs.

I nod. "Let's hope Fyodor sticks his neck out so we can take a whack at it."

"Fuck. Yes. At least Skye is on light duty cause of the baby. Still worries me when you're all out on a call. You can't control something like that."

"True, but it's okay because Cap is on her ass

all the time about sitting on her ass. She's allowed to drive and then sit." I laugh.

"Hey I heard that. I don't think my having to sit on my ass is a funny thing." Schuyler frowns as she joins us in the kitchen.

Sebastiano hands her a fresh cup of coffee. And gets a thermos ready for her.

"Seriously? Decaf? The doctor said I can have a regular cup of coffee." She whines.

"Sorry, baby. Decaf or no coffee. And no cheating at work. Nico won't keep secrets."

I try to give them my best 'don't involve me' look. But I think I failed because Sebastiano is smirking at me and Schuyler is glaring at me.

"You know you're my bodyguard and that means you're supposed to defend me, right? I may have to talk to Mira about the man she's choosing to be with."

I laugh more as I listen to her. This is the same conversation we have every work day since they found out they're expecting. It's become my morning entertainment.

"We should get going," Schuyler huffs.

Sebastiano grabs her and kisses her. "I love you both. Have a good shift."

I head to the car to warm it up and wait for Schuyler. She works a twenty-four hour shift and then forty-eight hours off. It's a weird schedule and it took me a few months to get used to it. But now it's better, the only thing I hate now is leaving Mira.

Mirabelle

I keep telling myself that there's nothing to worry about. Going back to class is the right thing to do. Life has to keep going, I just hate the unknown. I also don't think that they'll come after me, I don't matter to them. But my Nico...he definitely matters to them. And I know now that I can't live without him.

Doing my morning routine seems so lonely since Nico left earlier. I know I fell back asleep, but it's like my body knew he was gone. And the whole time I tried to sleep, I tossed and turned so much I finally just got up. Time to face the world again.

"Morning," I say to Marcello and Armando.

"Hey, morning." Armando smiles as Marcello grunts at me.

"He's never been a morning person." Armando laughs.

"I never was either. In fact, I'd rather have all

my classes in the afternoon. After this semester, I'll try to do that."

That gets me a thumbs up from Marcello. He's definitely not a morning person.

"I saw Alfonso's schedule and most of his classes are in the building next to mine. We won't have to move around too much," I say to them both.

"Are all your classes in the same building?" Armando asks.

"For this semester, yes. Usually they're not, but I got lucky."

"That's good, especially with this situation. Also, Carmelo and one of the MC brothers, Cavallo, will be around to help. Don't worry, we'll do our best to blend in."

I snort. "You guys can't blend in. You're huge."

That gets them both laughing. I don't think there's any man within our families that would be considered 'small.' My Nico is six foot four and at least two hundred and fifty pounds. Plus they're all covered in tattoos. 'Blend in'—that's funny.

"Fine. We'll do our best." Armando laughs.

We watch Alfonso trudge his way into the kitchen and take Marcello's cup of coffee that he just set down. Which makes Marcello growl at him.

"Get your own cup you lazy ass," Marcello grunts at him.

"Why? This was closer." Alfonso smirks as he finishes the cup and gets more.

"Brat." Marcello frowns and gets a new cup. Then he pushes Alfonso out of the way and gets more coffee.

I giggle watching them. It's a good start to my morning. I get my phone out to text Nico.

> Mirabelle: Morning, handsome.
> Getting ready to leave soon
> (Picture of his brothers)

> Niccolò: Morning, baby. Please
> be safe

> Mirabelle: I will. Armando said
> Carmelo and Cavallo will be with
> us too. Shouldn't you have extra
> help too?

> Niccolò: I'm okay, it's only on calls
> that I have to be more vigilant

> Mirabelle: I worry (sad face emoji)

> Niccolò: I worry about you too,
> Squeak. But I promise, I'll be okay,
> Schuyler will be okay. Besides, I
> have Cap and Rhys here too. Cap
> knows a little of what's going on.
> We're safe, the station is even
> closed to visitors for now

Mirabelle: Ugh. I still think you need extra help

Niccolò: How about this, if things get worse, I'll ask for extra help

I sigh as I read Nico's texts, I know he can handle himself. But that's really not the point. He's alone if anyone comes after him, and I don't like that.

Mirabelle: Fiiine. (pouting emoji)

Niccolò: Come down to the station when your classes are over. I want to see you

And then he says stuff like that and I'm smiling again.

Mirabelle: I will. I'll text you later (kissing emoji)

Niccolò: (kissing emoji)

Niccolò

I hate that Mirabelle is so worried about me. The reason that my brothers have extra help is because of how big the University campus is. So they need an extra set of eyes to help them. I just hope nothing happens, Fyodor is a slimy bastard, and he doesn't care if it's women or children he hurts. I look forward to when I'll be able to watch that light leave his eyes. He took my papà from my family and in return, I will take him from this world.

Days at the firehouse are usually pretty calm. We get our share of calls, but usually they're on the mild side. But then there's the bad ones and those stay with me. I'm just glad they're not the normal calls. So far today has been fairly slow, I don't say that out loud because I know about the jinx. You don't say easy days out loud or it'll turn into a shitshow.

"So tell me the truth, do I need to be worried about my girls?" Captain Michael Jeffries asks me.

I look over at him and think about what I can tell him.

"You want the truth? Are you sure?"

"Fuck yes, I want the truth," he barks out at me.

I nod. "Should you be worried? Maybe." I put my hand up before he can yell at me again. "I say maybe because I can't honestly say she's in any danger. This situation is between Southside and the Russians. The Mancinis and Cimaruta are our allies, so that makes everyone in some sort of danger."

"Then maybe my girls should come and stay with me and Lynn."

"If that's what you want, we can make that happen. But my brother Marcello and I would have to stay too."

"Why? I can keep my kids safe."

I know he understands why I protect Schuyler. And I also know why he feels like he can protect them too. Cap and his wife Lynn took Schuyler and Mirabelle in after Schuyler became a firefighter/EMT. So his view is from a father's view.

"I know you can, but you also know there's a reason that I'm Schuyler's bodyguard. And now my brother Marcello is Mirabelle's. That part of their life will never change, no matter what."

Cap frowns and sighs. "I just feel like I'm failing them again. I need to help keep them safe."

"You are. You make sure that Schuyler is safe when she's at work and every time both girls are with you. Trust us to take care of them the rest of the time."

I watch the emotions that are running through him. He finally nods at me.

"I do trust you and Sebastiano. And in time I'll trust your brother. But they're my babies, Lynn and I were never able to have our own. Then Schuyler came to us, bringing Mirabelle with her. They were the answer to our prayers and I failed Skye when I didn't save her from Blaine."

"You didn't fail anyone. If that's how you're going to look at it, then I failed her too. But we both know that neither of us failed her. We did the best we could in the situation."

Cap frowns, then nods. "Logically I know this. But my dad heart feels that sadness still."

I nod and stay quiet. Sometimes we just need to sit with our thoughts.

Chapter Nine

Mirabelle

"Hey, Mira!" I hear a voice call out to me. I turn towards it and see Darcy. The same Darcy that was a raging bitch in high school. Why the fuck is she talking to me?

"Who is that?" Marcello asks.

I quickly explain who she is and what she was like in high school. Marcello is frowning, I don't blame him, I'm pretty sure I'm frowning too.

"Oh. Hey, Darcy. I didn't know you were here in school."

She laughs this high-pitch, giggly laugh. It's annoying and I've never seen her act like this.

"I'm pretty sure I told you that I was going to the same University as you. I'm so excited to see you, who's your friend?"

Ohhh. Now I get it. It's not me she wants to talk to, it's Marcello. Which means she's still the same bitch she was before. Great. I look at Marcello, he's glaring at Darcy. I don't think she notices that he's doing that. She's still smiling at him and inching closer to him.

"Um. This is Marcello. Marcello, this is Darcy."

She gets even closer to him. "You're seriously hot." She looks at me. "Is he your boyfriend?"

"That's none of your business," Marcello says to her. "We need to get going."

He's not lying, my next class starts in fifteen minutes.

"I'll walk with you! I just finished my last class. Maybe we can hang out?" She asks.

"I have class, so I can't," I say as Marcello is leading me towards my next class. Darcy is almost running to keep up with us.

"We have so much to catch up on," she says from behind me.

I sigh softly and roll my eyes. I know she doesn't give a rat's ass about me, but what she doesn't seem to get is that Marcello wants nothing to do with her.

"Maybe another day," I say to her.

"I'm beginning to think she's not going to take the fucking hint," Marcello whispers to me.

"I don't think she will. If you want, I can skip my class and we can go find Armando."

"No, you need to be in class. I can handle that weirdo. Go. I'll be right here."

I nod. "Thanks."

It feels good to know that my education isn't just important to me. That I have people behind me, pushing me along. Sometimes I need that.

When I get out of class, I see Darcy is still talking to Marcello. He still has that annoyed look on his face. And he has company, Alfonso and Armando are with him and staring at Darcy.

"Mira! Finally. It's lunch time. Let's go," Armando says when he sees me.

I laugh and walk over to them.

"Nico wanted us to come by and see him," I say to them.

"How about I join you?" Darcy says, inviting herself.

I look at the three brothers and their faces are saying no.

"Maybe another day, Darcy. We already had prior plans and we can't change them," I say to her.

"Oh. Well, okay. Do you have classes tomorrow? We can hang out before or after."

I really don't want to be anywhere near her. And I don't understand her sudden interest in me. Except that she likes Marcello.

"Um. We'll see."

"We really need to go," Alfonso says.

I wave at Darcy as the three of them pull me towards the parking lot.

"She's fucking psycho. She kept asking about you and what you're doing now. And she kept touching Marcello," Armando says after we all get in the car.

"Yeah, she spent the last three years we were in high school bullying me. I don't understand why she's even talking to me now."

"There's something off about her. I just can't put my finger on it," Marcello says.

"We should have Sebastiano look into her and maybe even her family," Armando says.

Marcello gets his phone out and calls Sebastiano and tells him about Darcy.

"What did she do to you in high school?" Armando asks me.

"Just your normal bullying and harassing, I honestly just did my best to ignore her."

"I'm guessing you didn't tell Schuyler about what she was doing?"

"There was nothing to tell." I frown at him.

The silence that follows is almost deafening. What was I supposed to do? Go crying to my big sister because some asshole was picking on me? Please.

Mirabelle: We're on our way to the station

Niccolò: We're out on a call, but we'll be back soon. I can't wait to see you

Mirabelle: I need a Nico hug

Niccolò: What happened???

Mirabelle: Nothing really, just someone from my past that popped up today. It's made me feel weird and your hugs always make things better

Niccolò

I hate to think someone hurt my girl. It makes me irrationally angry and I want to kill whoever has done that to her. From what Marcello texted me, this bitch has been harassing Mira since high school. The shitty part is that I don't think she's ever told Schuyler about it. And I'm not going to be the one to tell her. When it comes to Mirabelle, Schuyler is very protective. I don't think she would've let it go. Because from what Mira told my brothers, the school did nothing.

Marcello is pulling into the firehouse parking lot just as we get back from the call. I jump out of the truck and go over to them to open the door for Mira.

"Wow. You don't open the door for me?" Alfonso laughs.

"Nope. You're not as pretty as my girl."

Everyone laughs as we head into the firehouse. Cap comes over and wraps Mira in a bear hug.

"How's my girl?" He smiles at her.

"I'm good, Dad."

"School's good? I heard you're having issues with a girl from high school?"

Schuyler is closing in on them as he asks about the problem in school. Mira is watching her and she looks a little scared.

"Um. Not really a problem. She's just acting like we're besties and we're not."

"Why didn't you tell us about her before?" Cap asks.

"There was nothing to tell. She's just a dick."

I can tell Mira's trying to move the conversation along. But I'm not sure they're going to let her.

"If it was just a 'nothing' thing, why didn't you at least mention it to me? We talk about everything." Schuyler frowns.

Mira sighs. "Okay, fine. She was an asshole, and a bully. But she didn't just do it to me. She did it to a lot of us and it wasn't just her. She had her group that helped her make a lot of people's lives suck."

"You still should've told me, Mom or Dad. We could've helped."

"Really? How? I couldn't have my big sister coming to school to defend me. It would've been worse!"

Cap steps between the sisters. "Okay, that's enough. Next time, you need to talk to us. I don't like that you dealt with it alone."

Mira nods.

Chapter Ten

Niccolò

Two weeks and still nothing from Fyodor. He hasn't poked his head out at all and it's making me crabby. I want him to stick his neck out so I can end this shit. Everyone is more on edge because we don't know where he is. And I guess if you think about it, he's doing the smart thing. We're all going crazy trying to figure out where he is and when he's going to come at us. Even his crew is quiet.

Sebastiano took today off because Schuyler has doctor appointments. So Marcello and I have switched roles. He will go with them and I get to be with my Mira. She has school and this is the first time I'll be with her.

"Morning, love," I say as I kiss her.

"Morning." She yawns. "I'm really excited that you'll be with me today."

"Me too. I finally get to see how your day goes."

"My days are boring. Just class and walking."

I laugh. "It's definitely different than Schuyler's day."

"That's true. I remember when she first started at the station. I got to spend the day with her at work and of course I was an asshole. But she still tried to make is a good day for us. I'd give anything to spend the day with her at work again."

"You can always come down to the station. I'm sure Cap would be okay with that, he was just telling me how he misses you."

"I feel like I'm in the way when I'm there." She sighs. "I know I'm just whining, I want to, but yet I feel like I'm in the way. Ugh."

She's so fucking adorable. "You're never in the way, Squeak."

"Maybe after all this crap is done, I can do a ride-along. That would be really fun."

I nod. "That sounds like a plan. Now as much as I want to just stay in bed with you, we need to get going."

She slides her hand between us and grabs my cock.

"Fuck, Mira," I growl.

"I think we have a little time before we get in the shower," she says as she strokes my cock.

Who am I to say no to her? I pull her night shorts off and rub myself on her. Knowing we don't have a lot of time, I slowly push into her.

"Oh fuck, Nico," she moans.

"You're always ready for me, so fucking wet and tight," I whisper as she nods.

I can feel her pussy trying to strangle my cock as I move. I reach between us and rub her clit, that makes her grab my ass and I rotate my hips in between thrusts.

"I'm going to come," she gasps.

"Come for me, baby." I grunt as I hold myself back. "I want to feel you coming on my cock."

"Fuuuuuuck!"

I thrust one more time into her as I release my load. I can still feel her coming on my cock and it feels like she's milking every last drop out of me.

I kiss her as we lay there holding each other.

"I love you, MIrabelle," I say softly.

Her eyes fly open and stare into mine.

"I was so afraid to tell you that I love you. I

didn't want to scare you away," she says as she continues to look at me.

"Baby, you couldn't scare me away. I would chase you to the moon and back. You are it for me."

Tears are welling up in her eyes.

"I love you, Niccolò. More than you'll ever know."

We lie there for a few more minutes as I hold her tight. Now I really wish we could just stay here all day.

"Are you joining me in the shower?" she asks me.

"Is that a real question?" I laugh as I pick her up and carry her to the bathroom.

After another quickie, we finally get out of the shower and get dressed. We're only fifteen minutes late, that's better than most days.

Mirabelle

Sitting in class, all I can think about is that Niccolò said he loves me. He loves me. Holy shit. Even though I felt it, I never thought I would hear it from him first. I thought it would be a long time before he said it. Dammit. I missed my whole class, it's a good thing my professor puts his lectures online for us to watch later.

As I head outside, I see Darcy walking towards me. Fuck.

"MIRA!" she yells. "Wait up!"

"Who's that? Oh wait. Is that Darcy? She hasn't gotten the hint yet." Nico frowns.

"That's her and apparently not." I sigh.

"Whoa. How are you always surrounded by hot sexy men?" She puts her hand out to touch Nico. He pulls away before she can.

"Are you headed to class?" I ask her.

She giggles. "No silly, I saw you and realized I haven't talked to you in a few days. I missed you."

Are you fucking kidding me? She missed me? That's a crock of shit and I know it, I just wish I knew what she was up to. Besides trying to touch all the men in my life. I look up at Nico and he's still frowning at her.

"I don't think we've met. I'm Darcy." She bats her eyelashes at him.

"I'm Niccolò," he answers stiffly.

"You're taller than Marcello." She inches closer to him.

He backs away and stands behind me. And I'm pretty sure he's glaring at her.

"We should be going," he says to me.

I nod. "It was nice seeing you, Darcy."

"Wait! You said we could have dinner soon. How about tonight?"

"We can't tonight. Sorry," Nico answers for me.

"We? Are you together?" She looks back and forth between me and Nico.

"We need to go," he says again and he sighs.

"You're more than welcome to come." She smiles at him again.

I can feel the tension coming off of Nico.

"We'll figure out something soon. Sorry, but we really do have to go," I say to her.

Before she can answer, Nico is leading me away.

"She really is annoying. My brothers were telling me about her, I thought they were exaggerating. But they weren't. And that's the bitch that gave you hell for three years?"

"That's her. Which is why I don't know why she's acting like we're friends. Because we never were and we're definitely not now."

"Bastian is looking into her. There's something weird about her, especially if she's making it seem like you've been friends."

"Maybe she's just an asshole, she obviously likes you and Marcello." I frown. Jealous? Ugh I know I shouldn't be. But seeing Darcy flirt with my Nico made me mad.

"Are you jealous, Squeak? Because you have no reason to be. I would never touch her. Or anyone for that matter. I told you, you're it for me."

"I'm sorry. I know I shouldn't get jealous, but sometimes...girls like Darcy just make me crazy. Especially after what she did in high school. I want her to stop talking to me and go away."

Nico takes my hand and kisses it. "It's kind of sexy when you get jealous."

I giggle. "You're crazy. But I love you."

The smile that spreads on his face makes me smile more.

"I love you, Squeak."

I don't think I'll ever get tired of hearing him say that.

As soon as we got back to the house, Nico got called to a meeting back at the property. Because he's my guard today, I go with him. There's always something to do there, they even have otters to play with. I love it. They're the most adorable animals.

They make little chirpy noises while they come over to you and love on you. There are three otter families that live on the property. Francesco Bastianini, the sergeant-at-arms for the Cimaruta, brought them in for his daughter. It's the most adorable story.

The drive to the property is about an hour without traffic. But this is Chicago, there's always traffic. When we get there, Nico gives me a kiss and heads to the Cimaruta clubhouse. I go and search for my sister, she texted me while we were driving that she was here too.

"So how was your appointment?" I ask her.

"It was good, Peanut is getting bigger. The doctor says I should start to feel better with the morning sickness. But there's a chance it could last till I give birth. That would suck."

I laugh at her expressions. "That would suck. But fingers crossed that you feel better soon." I crouch down to her belly. "You need to be nice to your mama. We're all really excited to meet you, but we need your mama in a good mood too."

Schuyler starts laughing. "I think Peanut heard you."

"Peanut better listen to Aunty Mira," I tease.

"How are things with Nico?"

"He told me he loves me." I say softly.

Suddenly she grabs me in a bear hug. "That's the best thing I've heard today. I'm so happy for you, Mouse."

I hug her back. "I didn't think he would say that to me for a long time. And I was afraid to say it to him first."

She chuckles. "You know, now he's going to bring up the fact that he said it first."

"He would do that." I laugh.

"How are things in school?"

I know what she's hinting at, and I don't want her to think that I didn't trust her before. Plus we just talked about this with Dad.

"School's good. Classes are definitely harder than high school."

She sighs at me. "You know what I'm talking about. I need to know why you never told me about this Darcy person?"

"There's nothing to tell about her. She's just an asshole from high school."

"I heard she was more than just an asshole. Armando was telling Sebastiano about her. Asking him to do a check on her. What did she do to you? And don't you lie to me, Mouse."

"She liked to mouth off, that's all. She never touched me, just made comments and was a bully to not only me. And before you ask, I did report it to the school and they didn't do anything."

This makes her even angrier. "You should've told me, Mouse. No one deserves to be bullied. I don't care what the reason is."

"I'm sorry I didn't tell you about Darcy and what she was doing. I felt like since she wasn't hurting me physically, I could handle it. You've done so much for me, I didn't want to add to it."

"Let's get one thing straight, Mirabelle. You are never too much for me. You're one of the most important people in my life and I should've known someone was hurting you. Now tell me about this bitch. Armando said she's acting like you're best friends?"

"Yeah, a couple of weeks ago, she came running up to me, talking to me like we've been friends forever."

"We all think she's up to something. I wish we knew what it was."

"She keeps asking me to go to dinner and hang out. But I don't want to hang out with her. I mean, I get that people can change, but she's never even said she was sorry. She makes it look like nothing ever happened."

I'm trying not to get angry but the more we talk about it, the angrier I'm getting.

"You need to get through the feelings you have over this. I can see how much it affects you, if it helps, talk to me."

"I just wish I knew why. Why did she act like that with me in high school and why is she pretending to be my friend now?"

I'm almost yelling now and I have to take several deep breaths to calm down.

"I'm so sorry I didn't see what you were going through," Schuyler says softly.

"None of this is your fault, I should've told you then. But I wasn't the only one she was doing this to. And the school wasn't doing anything about it."

Schuyler sighs. "Maybe when you start working with Miss Janice, you'll be able to fix that."

Leave it to my sister to find a light in all the darkness. "That's a great idea. Maybe I'll be able to make sure my old school finally takes care of their students"

"You will. I know that you'll do whatever you set your mind to doing."

"Thank you for always being my cheerleader. You're going to be a great mama to peanut."

"And you're going to be the best aunty."

Chapter Eleven

Niccolò

"All of you know Salvatore Mancini is a detective with the Chicago police. I'm going to turn the meeting over to him," Elio says to everyone.

"So we've been hearing some things about Fyodor Koslov. He's been in hiding for a while and I've been trying to keep an ear out for any news. Well, it looks like he's back in Chicago. In fact, I think his crew is back with him too. We need to be on alert because I won't put anything past any of them. I also found out more about Fyodor. We thought he was Conrad Blackwells cousin. It turns out that they're half brothers, same mother, different fathers."

"We're already on alert, double guards and no one goes anywhere alone. And how did we not know this about Conrad?" Enea says. "He worked with us for years, he was on our fucking board of directors."

"I think Fyodor brought in more of the mafia from Russia. And I can't put any alerts out because he hasn't done anything yet. But it looks like his council is here too. I did see all their names on a flight into Chicago last week. As for Conrad? His father raised him here in Chicago and Fyodor grew up in Russia. The chatter we heard, they kept calling each other cousin."

"Okay, so it looks like he's planning something," Giacomo says. "Is there a way we could get someone into his organization?"

"We thought about that. But we don't have anyone that could blend in with them," Elio answers. "Fyodor doesn't allow 'non Russians' into his organization and he checks their ties to Russia."

"What the fuck." Fantasma, one of the Cimaruta enforcers rolls his eyes.

"And they're not above taking women and children. I don't want any of the young ones off property. I know that's not the best case, but it's the best way to keep everyone safe," Enea adds.

"What about the women that have to be at work or school?" I ask.

"We're going to double up on bodyguards. Right now Carmelo and Marcello are on Mira and Alfonso. I want to add one more with them. All the younger kids will still be homeschooled. And then there's Schuyler, I know you think you can do it alone, Nico. But I don't want that. So I need volunteers to be the extra."

"I'll help Carmelo and Marcello," Hollis 'Cavallo' Taylor, a Cimaruta enforcer, volunteers.

"I'll go with Nico," Mitchell 'Granchio' Harris, says. He's another enforcer. "I usually take care of Sebastiano and Francesco's daughters. But since they're staying on the property, I can help."

"Thank you both. Maeve Bastianini, Francesco's wife, hasn't decided if she'll go back to college this semester. So if she does, we will need another volunteer to go with her and Fantasma."

"We have the women and children protected. All the families and members of Mancini, Southside and Cimaruta need to be on the property. There's enough room for everyone. And for the members and councils, no one goes anywhere alone. I don't care if it's just to the fucking grocery store. No one goes alone," Giacomo says.

Everyone agrees with Giacomo. We've had our share of problems before and if this is what it's going to take to keep us safe? We have to do it.

Before I met Mira, I wouldn't have hesitated to hunt Fyodor down and kill him. But now? I know that if something happened to me, it wouldn't just affect my family. It would affect Mira too and I can't do that to her. That doesn't mean I won't kill Fyodor. Slowly.

After we finish our meeting, we head back out and I immediately zero in on Mira. I head over to where she's talking with some of the women in the families.

"Hey, beautiful," I say as I give her a kiss.

"Hi, sexy." She smiles.

"Is everything okay?"

"Everything is great. How was the meeting?"

"We got some things straightened out. Cavallo will be with all of you at school and Granchio will be with me at the station."

She nods and holds me. I wish I could reassure her that everything will be okay. But I can't.

Mirabelle

I know things are getting worse, we have more guards with us now. Cavallo kind of stays between the two buildings that Alfonso and I are in. And I can feel how tense Marcello and Armando are. Marcello has started to sit with me in class. He says it's safer in case we have to leave in a hurry. He doesn't want to have to search for me.

Darcy hasn't come around this last week. And for some reason it bothers me more that she isn't around to get in my space.

"Your classes are boring," Marcello whispers to me.

I hold in my laugh as we listen to my professor. There are a lot of women in here that spend class staring at Marcello. I know he notices, but he pretends not to. Imagine if they could see the tattoos covering his body, they'd never learn anything.

"Holy shit. How do you even concentrate? Some of your professors are fucking bo-ring."

Marcello laughs as we walk to my last class of the day.

"They're not that bad." I laugh. "You can't come in today, we have a test."

"I don't like that. Are you sure I can't?"

"Yeah, remember? I got that email from my professor? She said no outside people on test days. But you'll be right outside the door. Nothing's gonna happen."

Marcello keeps frowning and calls Cavallo to come and watch with him.

"I'll see you in an hour. Maybe sooner if I finish early," I say to him.

"Okay. You know the rules. And if you need me, I'll be right here."

"I know. I'll be back," I say as I walk into class and take a seat in the back. I usually sit in the back on test days. Makes it easy to get out of class first when I'm done.

Half way through my test, out of the corner of my eye, I see someone sit down next to me. I try to ignore the rude ass that moved seats in the middle of a damn test.

"When you're done, you're going to get up slowly and come with me," I hear a voice whisper to me. It sounds familiar, I look over and see Darcy. Fuck.

"I'm not going anywhere with you," I angrily whisper back. That earns a few shushes from my classmates and a look from my professor.

"If you know what's good for you, you'll listen. And if you make a scene or try to alert anyone, I promise you will lose your sister. And everyone you care about."

She has to be lying, how could she even get close to the property or my sister?

"Your stupid family killed my father."

"I don't even know what you're talking about. Now get the fuck away from me." I start to pull my phone out to text Marcello. Darcy snatches it away from me. I look around, trying to decide if I can make a big enough scene so that I can get outside to Marcello and Cavallo.

Darcy grabs my arm and digs her nails in. "Don't be a dumb bitch. You think I'm here alone? You make any stupid move and my guys will kill your two outside."

She knows how many are out there...could she be telling me the truth about all the rest? I try not to panic. I wish I had put the tracker in like Nico asked. Because I kept putting it off, I don't have one yet. I was supposed to get one tonight. I know it would've worked. It worked when Schuyler was taken. Niccolò will find me, no matter what it takes. I know he'll never give up.

As some of my classmates start to stand and turn in their tests, I get up too.

"At least let me turn this in and I'll go with you."

Darcy walks with me to turn my test in. My professor doesn't even look up. Then she leads me out the side door that is never used. Dammit.

"Why are you doing this?" I ask her as we walk out. There's a man waiting outside the door. He joins us and stays close to me. I'm guessing he's there in case I try to get away.

"Were you not listening? Or are you that fucking stupid? Your 'family' killed my brother and father."

"What the hell are you talking about? No one killed anyone."

"You really are a dumb bitch. My brother was Blaine Blackwell. Well, half brother. Our father was Conrad Blackwell and I know for a fact that the Mancinis killed both of them. I also know that your boy, Nico and his 'family' helped them do it. So now? You're going to pay for what they did."

Holy fuck. This is about that woman beating asshole, Blaine? She's not wrong, Blaine and Conrad were killed. I don't know who killed them, but I know they're dead. Blaine not only beat my sister, his father had her kidnapped. They deserved to die. And I'm glad we got our revenge.

I look at her with the most innocent look I can muster up.

"I don't know what you're talking about," I say again.

"I know you know who they were. Blaine put up with your bitch sister for three years. She cheated on him many times and he took her back every time. He treated her like a queen and she walked all over him."

I snort as I listen to her. I tried to hold back, but listening to her spew that shit is fucking laughable. I feel something poking into my side.

"Laugh at me again and I'll make you sorry. Now move faster."

She shoves me into a car that's waiting. I feel a prick in my arm and everything starts to fade. My last thoughts are of my sister and Niccolò.

Chapter Twelve

Niccolò

We're in the middle of a call when my phone rings. I can see it's my brother, but I can't answer it right now. Being out in the open makes me nervous now that we know Fyodor is back. And my focus is on Schuyler.

Marcello: NICCOLÒ! For fuck's sake, answer your fucking phone!

Marcello doesn't usually yell so his text makes me panic and I call him back.

"What the fuck is going on? We're on a call and I can't answer all the time."

"She's gone. Fuck, fratello. I don't know how it happened. She was in class taking a test. We can't go in when they take tests. But when it was over, she never came out. And when I went to talk to her professor, she was gone too."

My heart feels like it's stopped. I had to have heard him wrong.

"What do you mean 'she's gone'? This is a joke, right?"

"Listen to me, Nico. I'm getting the school to get me any camera footage there is."

I feel like my world is spinning out of control. Not only is my heart missing, I have to tell her sister.

"Does Sebastiano know? He needs to be here when I tell Schuyler, she's pregnant, and this stress..."

"I called him already and he's on his way to you."

"Okay, I need to do something. But Schuyler's on shift till tomorrow morning."

"There's nothing we can do yet. I'll come to you as soon as I'm done here. I'm so sorry, Nico. I will find her."

"It's not your fault. I'll see you when you get here."

Now I need to pretend that nothing's wrong for Schuyler. I've never been so scared in my life, I know in my soul who took Mira. The question is, what are they going to do with her? I'm also angry at myself for not pushing her to get the tracker put in. We kept saying we would do it. She was set to get it done tonight and now she's gone. I'm going to kill anyone who puts their hands on my woman.

I hate that my brother feels like this is on him. This isn't on him, just like with Schuyler, there's nothing more he could've done. They got one on us and we need to adapt and find her.

After telling Cap and Schuyler about what happened, Cap gets moving on getting two firefighters to come in to sub for them. There's always someone who's willing to come in when there's an emergency. I overhear him calling Lynn and telling her what happened. And I can hear her scream from here. My heart hurts for them too.

I can't wait to get my hands on whoever took Mirabelle. I will make sure I watch the life drain from their eyes. And Fyodor? He will join Blaine and Conrad Blackwell in hell.

"Okay, we just have to wait for the ones taking our shift. Shouldn't be more than thirty minutes for the captain. We don't have to wait for both, just him," Cap says to me.

I nod at him. "I'm ready when you are. Everyone's back at the property waiting for Marcello to get the flash drive. We're hoping the cameras caught something on it."

"I thought your guys were watching Mira?" He frowns.

"They were. She was taking a test so Marcello couldn't go in with her today. And the back door that they made sure was never used...well, they used it."

Cap sighs. "I know it's not any of your faults

and I'm sorry for snapping. I'm just worried. Like I know you are too. You're going to find her right?"

"Hell yes we're going to find her. There's no option not to find her."

We see Cap's replacement come into the firehouse. I leave them so Cap can give him the updates. And I go and find Schuyler.

"Hey, are you ready to go?" I ask her. She's sniffling and that's my fucking kryptonite. Women I care about crying. I go over to her and hug her. "We're going to find her, Schuyler. I'm so sorry this happened."

"This is in no way your fault or anyone's except whoever took her. You will make sure they pay for this, right?"

"They will wish they never stepped foot near Mirabelle. I promise you that."

She nods and stands up, wipes her eyes and takes a deep breath.

"Let's find my Mouse."

Marcello

I don't know how they got past us. We've checked every entrance and exit in each of Mira's classes. We made sure that the door we're watching was the only way in or out. There is another one but it was sealed and not in use. Fuck! We made sure of it. I hated making that phone call to Niccolò. I've never seen my brother want to be with any woman. And now I've fucked up and lost her.

"Were you able to get the footage from around the building?" I ask Armando.

"Still waiting on the fucking IT guys. Sloths move faster than these assholes," he growls out.

We're all on edge waiting for what we need from the University's IT guys. Once we get the footage, we can take it to Francesco Bastianini. He and Sebastiano are our IT gurus. They will comb through the footage and find what we need. Then we can start looking for Mira. The pain I heard in my brother's voice was the worst. We've already suffered through losing our papà, we can't go through losing Mira. She's a part of our family. I just wish she had her tracker. Then we could just start with that, but she doesn't. So we need the IT guys to hurry the fuck up.

"Here's the footage. I didn't see anything weird on it. But my boss said I had to give it to you," one of the IT guy says to us as he rolls his eyes.

Armando takes the USB drive and stares at him. IT guy looks like he's going to cry.

"Let's get that to Francesco," I say before Armando can say what's on his mind.

We get back to the property in record time, and get the USB to Francesco.

Marcello: Did you tell Schuyler and Cap about Mira?

Niccolò: I had to, and it's fucking horrible. Their shift doesn't end till tomorrow. But they're trying to get the shift covered so we can leave.

Marcello: Okay. Should I go and pick up Lynn? Does she know?

Niccolò: Let me ask Cap.

I wait for Nico to get back to me. I can't believe I failed my brother and Mirabelle. How the fuck did this happen? All I know right now is that from now on? I will be in every fucking class that Mirabelle has. No more of this bullshit. Because we will find her, I don't care what it takes. She's coming home.

Niccolò: Cap said Lynn knows and if you could run to his place and pick her up, he would be really grateful. We'll be on our way as soon as the two backups get here.

Marcello: Okay, I'm heading out now with Fantasma and I'll see you when you get here.

I call Nico.

"What's up?" He answers.

"I needed to tell you how sorry I am. I wanted to do this when I saw you, but I also didn't want to wait. I don't know how they got by me. But fuck, fratello, I'm so fucking sorry."

"This isn't your fault, fratello. There's no blame here except to the ones who took my Mira. Not you. Never you."

"But she's my responsibility and I fucked up."

"No. I had to learn that when Schuyler was taken. There was nothing I could do then, and there was nothing you could've done for Mira. I love you, fratello. We'll find my girl."

"I love you too. And fuck yes, we'll find her."

I don't know how he's not blaming myself for this. I blame me for this. And if something bad happens to Mira? I know I couldn't live with that. Waiting for my brother and the rest of them to get here is almost as torturous as waiting for the assholes with the flash drive.

I head out to go and pick Lynn up, I just hope she doesn't hate me for this.

It takes me about fifteen minutes to get to Cap and Lynn's house. It's a gorgeous farmhouse-style home with a few acres. I get out of the car and knock on the front door. Lynn opens the door and embraces me.

"Is there any news yet?" she asks me as she grabs her things.

"No, nothing yet. We got the camera footage and hopefully there will be something on there."

"I have faith that you'll find her. Now let's get back to the property and see how I can help."

"I'm so sorry I let this happen."

"Marcello, you didn't let this happen. Please don't ever think we blame you. Or any of you. This is on who took her and no one else."

The relief I feel makes my body feel lighter. Knowing that her parents understand what our lives are like. Because it's going to be really stressful until we do. And it's easy to point fingers and blame.

Chapter Thirteen

Mirabelle

I peel one eye open and try to focus on my surroundings. I remember Darcy making me go with her, but the rest of it is fuzzy. I'm pretty certain that I was kidnapped. I don't feel like I'm hurt anywhere yet and I don't hear any voices around me. I know that Nico will find me, he won't stop till he does. He told me before that he would burn down the city to find me.

They took my watch and phone, so I have no idea how long I've been here. My hands are tied behind my back and my feet are bound together. They've left it slightly loose and I can move my hands and feet. But I can't get them out of the ropes. Just as I'm trying to wiggle my hands more, the door opens. I immediately stop and pretend to be sleeping still.

"Shouldn't she be awake by now?" I hear Darcy say.

Then I feel something slice my arm. It takes a lot to not move from the shock of it.

"Why isn't the bitch waking up?" Darcy asks the mystery person.

"Maybe you gave her too much," a deep voice says in a heavy Russian accent.

"Shut up. I didn't put the sedative together, you moron. Find a way to wake the bitch up. Fyodor wants to know what she knows about the Mancinis, the Cimaruta and Southside. In high school she was just a spineless baby. Now she thinks she's better because of who she hangs with. And she acts like she's with one of those guys? That's fucking laughable."

They both leave and I breathe a sigh of relief. I wish they had faced me to the door so I could've at least tried to get a look at the guy. I wonder if she was telling the truth about being Blaine's sister. We never even heard of her from him. He always said he was an only child. Could he have been lying to her from the beginning? Since he and his father are dead, there's no one we can ask that question to.

If Blaine was lying from the start, he was more of an asshole than I thought. I still wish I had known what he was doing to Squirrel. I had my suspicions but she hid it very well, I never saw any marks on her. I did see the way she looked at him towards the end. I'm glad he's gone.

But now I have to figure out how to make it out of this without shedding more blood. I like my blood inside my body and not outside. And I wish I knew what they wanted me for. It's not like I'm a part of the mafia or the MC. So what the fuck is going on? I say a silent prayer for Nico to find me. I miss him so much.

I don't know how long I was out, but now I can't shut my mind off. I take a few deep breaths and try to listen for sounds outside the door. Sadly I don't hear anything. I can feel myself getting drowsy again. I don't want to fall asleep, but I can't stop it.

The door bursting open scares the shit out of

me and as hard as I try, I can't stop my body from reacting.

"Oh good. You're finally awake," Darcy says as she comes over and stands in front of me.

"What do you want from me? I don't know why you think you can get anything from me."

"You're the key to me finding out what happened to my brother and my dad. And you're going to help me get the information I want."

I laugh at her. "I don't know what you're talking about."

She reaches out and slaps me.

"Don't laugh at me, you bitch. I know that you know what happened to them. Your sister is married to a Mancini. You all know what happened. So don't try to act all innocent and sweet. Because whatever happened to them? Is going to happen to you. None of you really knew who my dad was and if you did? You would've treated him better."

"Blaine went away on a trip and that's the last I saw of him. And your dad? He tried to kill my sister."

"Your sister is a whore and deserved what she got. We both know Blaine and my dad are dead. I just want to know who did it."

I stare at her with a blank look. Even if I did

know the details of what happened to them, I sure as fuck wouldn't tell her. Darcy punches me in the mouth and I spit my blood at her.

"Yeah, you're a big shot punching me with my arms locked up," I sneer at her. In the last few months, Nico and some of the other guys have been teaching us how to defend ourselves. I think I could definitely kick Darcy's ass. And if she'd take the restraints off that's what I'd do. I don't know how far I'd get after her, but it has to be better than sitting here letting her hit me. Fucking coward.

Darcy laughs. "You'll get your chance. And then you'll die. Oh, but not before we make sure your whore sister gets to watch you die."

She's fucking crazy. Finally, she stalks out of the room and I hear the lock click. I wiggle my hands again to try and get the knots to loosen. I don't know if it's working, but it does feel like it's getting looser.

Niccolò

It's been six hours since Mira was taken by Darcy. We've learned a lot about her since. She's the half sister of Blaine Blackwell, the bastard who beat Schuyler. They shared the same bastard father, Conrad. Darcy is six years younger than Blaine and we're not sure if he knew about her. But we know that Conrad did, we've uncovered pictures of him with Darcy. Now I'm wondering if Blaine being with Schuyler was all a set up of some sort. She got into the firefighters academy when she was eighteen and met Salvatore Mancini around that time. They became friends and then she met Blaine. Conrad also weaseled his way onto the Mancini board of directors with his money.

"How did we miss all of Conrad's connections with the Russians?" Enea frowns as he reads the information.

"When he came to us, we did the regular checks and nothing came up. We didn't do deep looks unless there were flags on them. And Conrad came up clean. No ties to any organization. Which now I know was a cover up. But we couldn't have known," Sebastiano says.

Enea sighs. "I know what you mean, son. It's just so fucking frustrating that we missed something like that. People got hurt because of it. It's on me. And that pisses me off."

"It's done and past. We can't change that, but we need to fix this now. And we will. First we need to get Mirabelle back and then we will take care of Fyodor and his crew," Giacomo says.

Francesco was able to get useful footage off of the USB drive. We saw Darcy and another man walking with Mirabelle. We see Darcy shove Mira into a car. And even though it's not crystal clear, we can see Mira slump over in the car. That one made Niccolò put his hand through a wall.

"Our next step is finding out more about Darcy. Where she lives, who she hangs out with....everything. Then we'll trail her, I'm doubting she's a criminal mastermind. So she'll fuck up at some point and I'm thinking it'll be sooner rather than later," Francesco says.

"How can I help? I need to do something." I'm not trying to be angry, but I fucking am. Not at anyone here, but at the bitch who took my girl and whoever is putting their hands on her.

Francesco hands me a computer. "I started a search on here and you can read what I've found on her so far."

"I'm going to send a few of my guys out to ride and scout. Starting at the area where we can see she was taken," Giacomo says.

"And don't forget the professor. She had to see what was happening when Darcy took Mirabelle. And she could be involved," Marcello adds.

"I'm on the professor, we have her name and address and I've got one of our men sitting on her house," Elio tells us. "He called to say she just got home. He'll be on her twenty-four seven until we find Mira."

"If her professor is really in on it, she needs to be fucking fired. She's endangered a student's life for fuck's sake," I snap.

"We will make sure she pays for it if she's a part of it," Elio says, coming over to hug me. "We're going to find her."

I know I'm not helping the situation, but it's hard to be calm when I don't know if they're hurting her. That's my biggest fear is what is she going through, will she be able to come back from whatever they do to her. I know she watched her sister recuperate when she was taken by Conrad. And I saw how hard that was for her. We need to find her. Now.

Chapter Fourteen

Mirabelle

I know it's been a few days since Darcy took me. They bring me breakfast, lunch and dinner. So that's how I've been judging how many days are passing. They should be bringing me lunch. At first I didn't eat, who knows what they're putting in it. But hunger and thirst won and I had to eat at least a little. There is a bathroom connected to this room and they let me roam between the two unrestrained. When they come in to bring food, one watches me and the other drops the food off. There's one that is more gentle with my restraints.

He doesn't say much but he doesn't seem to fit here with them. Maybe I can get him to help me.

When Darcy comes, they tie me back up. It's stupid. She never comes alone and I'm not an idiot. There's no way I could take the guys she brings in with her. So far she's tried to intimidate me by smacking me around. She doesn't hit like a normal person. It hurts, but yet it makes me want to laugh. I have realized that laughing at her makes her really angry. The last time I did it, the big ugly asshole that comes in with her had to carry her out. I spent a while laughing about that. Laughing helps me to keep my cool. I don't want to show any of them how scared I am. Because I'm fucking terrified. They haven't really done anything to me yet and I'm afraid that it's coming.

Today when they bring me lunch, the nice one comes in and ties my hands up and handcuffs my leg to the bedpost. Great. That means bitchzilla is coming in. They bring my food in and she walks in after.

"You should eat today. Because it might just be your last meal. Today we're going to see just how valuable you are to the Mancinis." Darcy smirks at me. "It's going to be a great day."

I don't know what the fuck she means. Is she going to kill me in front of them? She can't be that crazy, can she? Maybe she's gonna try and trade me? Crazy bitch. Darcy walks out and the only nice one that comes over and takes my restraints off.

"Thank you," I say as I watch him.

He looks at me and nods. "You should eat," he says in a heavy Russian accent.

"Please help me. I don't know why Darcy is like this, it has nothing to do with Blaine or Conrad. She had it out for me way before."

He turns to me and frowns.

"I can't help you. I'm sorry."

"Please," I beg him. I can see scars littering his face and neck. What the fuck happened to him?

"You dumb fuck! Stop talking to that asshole and get out here. I need help!" Darcy screams at him. He takes a deep breath and turns to leave. Giving me one last glance. Maybe he'll change his mind and help me.

Niccolò

Three days. That's how long half of my heart has been missing. We've been watching the professor's house and so far she's left to go to class and that's it. But my gut is still saying she has something to do with this. Francesco is still digging into her. Darcy has holed up somewhere, I'm guessing it's wherever she's taken my Squeak. I've never been one to hurt women. Darcy is making me start to rethink that stance on women like her.

"Bosco called and said there's a woman that just got to the professor's house. And it looks like it's Darcy," Elio tells us.

"Cavallo and Lorenzo, you two go and back him up. Take the SUV, it's quieter," Enea says.

"Sí, Papà," Lorenzo answers. He and Cavallo head out.

Could this really be the key to finding Mira? Growing up Catholic, we prayed a lot. But I think these last few days I've prayed more than my entire lifetime. It's the waiting that's the worst.

"What is the plan if it is Darcy?" Marcello asks.

"We follow her, she has to go back to wherever she was. And I think wherever that is? It's where she has Mira," Elio says.

Everyone agrees with Elio.

"We still can't find Fyodor. Do you think he's holed up wherever they have Mira?" I ask.

"That's what I'm hoping. I'd like him to stick his ugly head out. He's a fucking coward."

Elio steps away to answer his phone, and we all wait for updates.

"Cavallo says that they're following Darcy. She seems to be pretty close to the professor, so I'm almost certain she knows what's going on."

For the first time since Mira was taken, I feel like we're on our way to finding her. And the first thing I'm going to do is get that damn tracker put in her. I don't care if I have to hold her down and do it myself.

Mirabelle

No one comes into the room after my dinner plate is taken. So hearing the lock click and the door opening makes me start to panic.

"Don't be scared," I hear the nice Russian say. "My name is Ivan, I am going to try to help you. But you have to be quiet, Fyodor will kill both of us if he catches us."

Fyodor. I heard that name before, he's the head of the Russian mafia here in Chicago. I remember hearing that they originally thought Fyodor and Conrad were cousins. Then they found out they are half brothers, they have the same mother. Such a fucked-up family.

Ivan unties my hands and gets the cuff off my leg.

"You follow behind me, other guards are sleeping."

"Where's Darcy? She won't let me go," I whisper.

"She left. But we need hurry, she be back," he says.

I grab the back of his shirt and follow him out of the room. After walking down a short hallway, there's a huge room. I thought we were in a house, but now I think it's a warehouse. It's way too big to be just a house. We keep near the wall and make our way to another door.

"Ivan, what are you doing?" We hear a voice call out.

I keep myself right behind Ivan, he's so big I'm hoping that whoever that is, won't see me.

"Can't sleep, taking a walk," he answers.

Ivan's answer must make sense to whoever that is, because he leaves. I can hear his footsteps getting farther away. We're almost to the front door when the door to our left opens.

"Ivan. What are you doing?" A man with a thick Russian accent says.

"Fyodor—I was taking her outside to get air."

"You know better than that." The man pulls a gun out and shoots Ivan.

I scream as arms grab me and drag me back to the room I was in. This time they handcuff my hands and feet to the bed. And I do my best to curl up as I sob. Ivan was just trying to help me and now he's dead.

"You made me kill one of my best men. I don't know how you got him to help you, but know this. No one else will be helping you. And no one's coming to rescue you," Fyodor says to me.

I feel him sit on the bed and he runs his hand on my body. Please don't let him touch me. I try to stop crying, but I can't. All I can think of is the look on Ivan's face as he fell. I take a deep breath and hold it as Fyodor brings his face to mine.

"Don't worry, I'll show you how a woman should be treated. You'll pay for what you made me do tonight."

I slowly let my breath out as he gets up and leaves. I hear the lock click. This time he didn't touch me, but what about the next time?

Chapter Fifteen

Niccolò

Cavallo calls to tell us that they followed Darcy back to a warehouse out in the industrial area of South Chicago. We're all getting ready to meet them there. The tension is so thick that you can feel it in the air.

"I want to go with you," Cap says to Elio.

"I don't think that's a good idea."

"Why? I can handle a gun and I can take care of myself."

"It's not that. It may come down to killing. We will not hesitate to kill any of them that are standing in the way of us getting Mirabelle back and capturing Fyodor."

Cap takes a deep breath. "I can do it."

"Mira will need you here. Your wife and Schuyler need you here," Elio says to him.

"Then I need to look that man who took her in the eye. You promise me that I'll get to confront him."

Elio thinks and then looks at Enea and Giacomo. They nod at him.

"Okay, Cap. You will be there when we bring him back," Enea says.

"Thank you."

I'm a little worried about Cap being there when we bring Fyodor back. I don't think he's ever seen this side of what we do. But I do understand why he wants to be here. Fyodor will die and it'll be by my hand.

"Everyone understands that Fyodor is not to be killed. He is to be taken alive no matter what," Elio says. "His connection to Southside is more than any of you know. And I think I need to explain it."

Elio looks at me and my siblings, then goes over to my mamma and wraps his arms around her.

"As most of you know, Agostino Marini was shot and killed nineteen years ago. He was out to dinner with his family. We never knew who did it because the shooters wore masks like the cowards they were. But now we know who did it, and we even know who pulled the trigger and why. Fyodor Kaslov was the one who killed Agostino. He did it as his initiation for their crew. At the time, it was his father running the Russian mafia and I had just taken over from my papà. Agostino was my consigliere which is why Fyodor targeted him."

There's an audible gasp from everyone. I look over at my mamma and see her tears falling. I go over to her and hug her.

"I will get revenge for Papà," I whisper to her. "Fyodor will not get away a second time."

My mamma embraces me tightly.

"I need you to be safe, Niccolò. I can't bear to lose any of you."

"You won't lose us, mamma."

"Now you all know why we need Fyodor alive. We want him to confess to what he's done. That's when we will get our revenge and close this chapter of our lives."

Everyone says yes to Elio, I can see the sadness in some of their faces after hearing our story. I think my papà would be proud of all of us. In fact, I'm positive he would be. I can't wait to close this chapter of our lives. And start the next one with Mirabelle.

While we are getting ready, Carmelo, Fantasma and Sebastiano have gone out to get the professor and bring her back here. She has a lot to answer for.

There's so many of us, it takes four SUV's to get us to the warehouse. We keep our distance when we meet up with the guys that have been waiting. I feel like my body is vibrating, my Squeak could be in that building. And we have to find a way to keep her safe.

"The fucking building is metal so our thermals aren't doing well to see inside," Cavallo says quietly. "And we heard a gunshot about fifteen minutes ago. No one's come out yet."

We're quietly discussing how we're going to get in there. Cavallo and Lorenzo have been here since following Darcy from the professor's house.

"We can see that there's quite a few men in there. From what I saw, there's at least thirty in there. And I saw at least ten walking around the property. There's a few cameras I can see, on the building. So if they're on, they'll see us coming," Lorenzo says.

"Can we somehow loop their feed?" Enea asks.

"Only if I can find their main line and tap into it. But I doubt it because it's probably all inside the building," Sebastiano answers.

"Everyone get your suppressors on. We can take out the ones outside first and then deal with the ones inside as we get in."

I start to open my mouth and Elio puts his hand up.

"I know, Niccolò, we are going to be as careful as we can. We don't know the layout of the building, we're doing our best."

Fuck. I know everyone is. But that's my whole world in there, and I will kill anyone that gets in my way of finding her.

"Do you think we can cut their Wi-Fi? That would bring down their cameras and if we're lucky, they may not notice right away. Or we might get super lucky and they won't have anyone watching the cameras," Francesco says to Sebastiano.

"That might work. Worst case they'll know and come out shooting. So we need to make sure everyone is ready before we cut the Wi-Fi. And maybe take the guards out first."

"Sounds good," Giacomo says.

We all start to spread out, making sure the coms are working.

We're coming, baby.

Mirabelle

It takes a while but I finally get myself to calm down. Maybe Ivan isn't dead? I can't handle the fact that Fyodor shot him because he was helping me. He didn't have to shoot him. My tears start flowing again as the door opens.

"You dumb fucking bitch!" Darcy screams. "You got Ivan killed."

Right as I turn to look at her, she swings something at my head and everything goes black.

When I wake up, my arms and legs are splayed open, tied to the bed posts.

"Oh good, you're finally up. Did you have a good sleep, princess?" Darcy sneers at me. "Now you're going to pay for getting Ivan killed."

The door opens again and Fyodor walks in, he's wearing a robe.

"I'll leave you two alone." Darcy giggles. "Have fun, you two."

I say a silent prayer to my Niccolò, please find

me. I can survive anything as long as I can get back to him.

"You are a pretty little thing." Fyodor smiles at me as he takes his robe off.

I breathe a little sigh of relief when I see he's not totally naked. He walks towards me, sits on the bed and runs his hand down my body.

"You made me kill one of my best men tonight. And that's not something I can just let go," he says as he rips my shirt open.

As hard as I try not to, a tear slips out. He wipes my tear with his finger and licks it off as he smiles at me. He starts rubbing himself through his boxers. Then he reaches over to me and pulls my shorts down. I don't even know where this shirt and shorts came from.

My mind goes back to Niccolò. I wasn't a virgin when I met him, but he's the only one I want touching me. More tears are falling as I watch Fyodor. I can survive anything.

"Jesus, you are gorgeous," he rasps out as he gets the rest of his clothes off and strokes his cock.

Niccolò

After we take care of the guards walking around, Francesco cuts the Wi-Fi. We slowly make our way to the doors, there are two. And we have men at both of them. We considered kicking in the doors, but with that many men in there? That's a sure way to get our guys shot and maybe even Mira.

When we get our door open, we can hear snores coming from the closest room. And footsteps coming from somewhere else. I take the first room, quietly slicing cleanly through the guard's jugular and carotid arteries. He didn't have enough time to realize what happened. Next we take out two that are watching TV, again we're able to take them out fast and quiet. No bullets, just clean and swift.

"Three down, security and one room. Going to check each door now," Lorenzo says quietly into our coms.

"Five down here, no rooms yet. No bullets unless absolutely necessary. And we need Fyodor. Any sign of him or Darcy?" we hear Elio ask everyone.

"Nothing yet. But they have to be here. No one's left from my side of the building," Carmelo says from his lookout.

"No one's left from my side either," Domenico Mancini says from his.

Five minutes later and five more Russians taken down. There's still quite a few more doors to go and we haven't seen Fyodor or Darcy. The problem is not killing them, I want both of them gone. Now.

We get to the last door in this hallway and I slowly open the door. What I see makes my blood run cold. Fyodor is stroking himself as he looks at my Mirabelle. I run in and tackle him to the ground. My fist connects with his face and I feel his nose break. I keep hitting him. Marcello grabs me and pulls me off Fyodor as Amante cuffs him.

"Snap out of it Niccolò! Your girl needs you," Marcello says to me.

I shake my head to try and clear it. Mira. I turn and walk over to her.

"Nico," she sobs.

I get the cuffs off of her and gather her in my arms.

"I knew you'd find me." She sobs harder.

"Shhh. Breathe baby. I got you," I whisper as I hold her. I hold her as her sobs shake her whole body.

Marcello hands me a quilt that I use to wrap Mira in.

"We have Mirabelle and Fyodor," I say quietly into our coms.

"We have Darcy," Enea says back. "Everyone get back to the cars. Be aware that we got as many of Fyodor's crew as we could. Taking a few back with us. But from what they're saying? There's more of them that aren't here."

"Got it. We'll see you at the cars."

I gently pick Mira up and hold her tightly to me.

"I love you, Squeak," I whisper to her.

"I love you." She sniffles.

We get back to the cars and head back to the property. Enea calls ahead to let everyone know that we have Mirabelle. And as much as I don't want to leave her, I will have to. I need to take care of Fyodor and the rest of his crew. But tonight? Tonight no one can make me leave her. I need to make sure she's okay and that we got there before Fyodor could touch her. And if he did? I will make him suffer more.

Chapter Sixteen

Niccolò

Mira's scream jolts me out of my sleep. My arms are still wrapped around her.

"Shhh. It's okay, Squeak. You're safe," I whisper to her.

I can feel her heart racing and her body is shaking.

"Nico?" she asks, sounding confused.

"It's me, baby. You're home and safe."

She starts crying as I hold her.

"I dreamt that I was still in that room and Fyodor was coming for me."

"He's never going to come near you again. I promise you that."

I hold her until her breathing evens out, telling me that she's finally fallen asleep again. Fyodor is going to pay for doing this to my Mira. I lay here and think of all the ways I'm going to make him pay. For my papà and for my girl.

When I wake up in the morning, I spend some time watching Mirabelle sleep. She's the most beautiful woman I've ever laid eyes on. We haven't talked about her being taken yet. But I have to know what happened before I see Fyodor. I need to know what he did to her. I close my eyes and hold her.

"Morning, Nico," I hear her say.

"Morning, love. How are you feeling?"

"Better. I knew you'd come for me, all of you."

"I would burn the world down to find you, Mira. Don't you ever doubt that. I need to ask you a few things, and I know it's not going to be easy. But I have to know."

She looks at me and nods. I ask her what happened, why she left with Darcy. What happened while she was in that room. And the hardest question, *did* Fyodor touch her. She answers all my questions as her voice shakes. When she gets to my last question, her tears start to fall. She tells me how he started to touch her, but we got there right before he could do anything. The relief that floods my body is incredible. Fyodor's still going to suffer for putting her through this.

"I don't want to leave you, but I have to for a while today. But all the women will be here with you. You won't be alone."

"Are you going to take care of Fyodor and Darcy?"

I debate on how to answer that. But I realize there's no point in lying to her.

"Yes."

"Can you make sure he suffers for killing Ivan? He tried to help me escape and because of that, Fyodor shot him. It's my fault Ivan died."

"That wasn't your fault, baby. But yes. I will make sure he knows it's for Ivan too."

We get up and grab a shower together. I want to make love to her and help erase the bad shit she's gone through. But I'm letting her take it at her pace. I won't force her to do anything. Not even when it comes to healing. That will come in time, I know I'll wait forever for her.

After making sure that Mira is surrounded by all the women, I head to the clubhouse. The basement is where we take people for interrogation. The clubhouse is filled with all the guys waiting to see what's going to happen. We got some good news while we were rescuing Mira— Anthony woke up from his coma and they expect him to make a full recovery.

I see Elio, Giacomo and Enea. I head over to them.

"Are we ready to go down and talk to Fyodor?" Enea asks when he sees me.

"I've been ready since I saw him in that fucking room," I growl out.

"I think we should talk to Darcy first. Let Fyodor sit for a while," Giacomo says.

We can't all go down to the basement, so we decide that Elio, Giacomo, Enea, Sebastiano, Francesco, Marcello and I will go. It's also decided that when it's time to take care of Fyodor, my brothers will be with me.

The underground area of the clubhouse is huge. It's bigger than the main area of the clubhouse. From what Giacomo told me, the founders of the Cimaruta built this building to store the guns and drugs that they used to run. That was how the Cimaruta made money when they first came here from Italy and Ireland. Now they're legit and trying to clean up the streets of Chicago. In fact, that's what all of us are doing.

I open the door to the room that Darcy is chained up in.

"You can't chain me up like I'm a fucking animal!" she screams at us.

We all laugh at her. I start walking towards her, Enea holds me back.

"Be careful, you don't want to get too close, she's a spitter."

I stop walking and look at Darcy.

"You mean like you chained up Mirabelle?" I snap at her.

"That whore deserved everything she got. I know Fyodor had a lot of fun with her." She smirks at me.

"Tell us what you have against Mirabelle," Enea says.

"I don't have anything against her. She's just a spineless bitch. Just like her sister. Schuyler treated my brother, Blaine, like a piece of shit and someone had to pay for his disappearance. I chose Mira and she deserved everything Fyodor did to her."

Hearing Darcy say that Fyodor touched my woman is making me see red. Mira told me that he didn't touch her. Could he have done it while she was passed out? Either way, I'm going to make his last hours slow and painful.

"I think it's funny that you think you're going to win this battle. Our family will never let this go." Darcy laughs.

After we finish up with Darcy, it's time to take care of Fyodor.

"What are we going to do with her? If we let her go, she's not going to just walk away. And now that we know she's directly tied to Fyodor? We definitely can't let her go," Enea says.

"We don't know how important she is to the Russians," Elio says.

"So we just keep her here for now. Until we can get the information we need." Enea sighs.

"There's no other options." Giacomo sighs.

He's right. We really don't have any other options. Well, the other option is to kill her, and that's not what we do. Or...that's not what we usually do.

I take a deep breath before opening the door to the room that contains Fyodor. His face is swollen from when I beat on him at the warehouse. He looks up at me.

"Your girl was delicious. Maybe you can bring her in for one last time. I mean, you are going to kill me, right? At least let me fuck her one last time."

Giacomo steps in front of me. "He's trying to goad you into losing it. Don't let him win, you're better than this."

Fyodor laughs. "Fuck you all. I won. You lost. You can do whatever you want to me and you'll never get rid of my family."

"I'm glad you still think so highly of your family. Most of them are dead, and the rest are in hiding. And if they're smart? They won't ever show their faces in my city again. We're going to make sure everyone that has your blood flowing through their veins disappears," Enea says to him.

"Bullshit. We're already here, you never even suspected Conrad. He was with you for years. Right under your fucking nose, reporting back to me." Fyodor laughs more.

I take the knife on the table and stab it through his hand. He screams and that makes me smile. I pull the knife out and stab through his other hand.

"Don't play with the asshole." Sebastiano chuckles.

"That's not playing. This is playing." I pick up

the gun on the table and shoot Fyodor through his left knee. "That's for touching the one pure thing in my world."

"Fuck! I lied, okay? I didn't touch her," he spits out.

"Well that's a lie. You may not have fucked her, but I know you touched her."

"I did not touch the bitch!"

I shoot through his other knee.

"Call her a bitch one more time," I snap.

Carmelo and Armando step into the room. Each one picks out a weapon and walks over to Fyodor. They take turns using their weapon of choice on him. I can see the rage and anger on their faces. I was five when he killed our papà, my brothers and I are all two years apart. They have a more vivid memory than I do of that night.

Finally Elio stops my brothers, Fyodor is barely conscious.

"Tell me why you killed our papà," I say to him.

"I did nothing to your papà," he slurs out.

"Agostino Marini. You killed him in front of his family."

Fyodor starts coughing up blood and making a wheezing noise. I think he's trying to laugh.

"Fuck Marini. He was a coward and deserved to die."

I point the gun and shoot him through his stomach. I don't care if he doesn't tell me why. I know why. Killing my papà made him the head of the Russian mafia. I can't wait any longer. I raise my gun one last time and shoot him through his forehead.

It took nineteen years, but my papà has been avenged. And the man that took him from us and tried to hurt my girl is dead. He'll never hurt anyone ever again.

Epilogue

Mirabelle

It's been one month since Darcy kidnapped me. The professor that helped her has been fired and stripped of all her teaching credentials. We found out that she was Darcy's mother. Sebastiano and Francesco are updating our security everywhere. From the cars we drive, to the homes we live in. I also had my tracker put in. I don't ever want to be in a position where no one knows where I am.

I roll over in bed and snuggle with Nico. I thought I loved him before all this happened. How I feel about Nico now is so much more than before.

He is my life, he's a part of my soul. He treats me like I'm the most important person in the world.

"Morning, handsome," I say as I nibble on his chest. I can hear him growl, and the rumble in his chest is making me wet. I moan softly.

Niccolò

Waking up to Mirabelle is the only way I ever want to wake up. And waking up to her biting on my chest? Fucking heaven.

I take one of her nipples into my mouth and swirl my tongue around it, getting that soft moan I love to hear. I move on to her other breast and get a louder moan. I make my way down her body and capture her clit gently between my teeth, then soothing it with my tongue.

"Nico," she gasps.

I slide a finger in her, curling it to reach her g-spot. Which sends her over the top. I smile as I feel her coming and I suck her clit harder.

"Holy fuck, Nico," she pants.

I line the head of my cock up with her and slowly push in. I still myself as she adjusts to me, she's so fucking tight.

"You were made for me," I whisper to her as I start to move. I've learned this is heaven and I don't ever want to leave. I move faster.

"I'm going to come, Nico," she moans.

"Come with me, baby."

I reach between us and circle her clit, I feel her squeeze my cock as she's coming.

"Fuck, yes," I growl as I empty myself deep in her. I wrap my arms around her and hold her to me. "I love you so fucking much."

Mira pulls back a little to look at me.

"I love you so much. Thank you for rescuing me."

"I told you, I would burn the fucking world down to find you."

Tonight is another Cimaruta barbecue, and it's a special night. Well, it will be a special night. I can't explain it, but I can find Mirabelle in any crowd. She's like a beacon for me, my North Star that helps me find my way home. I make my way over to her. And get down on one knee.

"Mirabelle, my Squeak, you are everything to

me. My heart, my soul, my compass that points me to be the best man I can. Marry me?"

Mira has tears in her eyes. "Yes, Niccolò. There's nothing more I could want than to be your wife. You are my soulmate and I can't wait to spend the rest of our lives together."

I stand and place the ring on her finger. Then I pick her up, spinning her around. She squeals as she holds onto me.

Everyone cheers and comes over to give us hugs and congratulations.

Mirabelle

"Just so you know, I don't want a long engagement. And I will finish school, but I have to tell you something and I hope you're as happy as I am."

Nico puts me down gently and looks at me.

"Tell me."

I hand him the pregnancy test I took this morning.

"Is this what I think it is?" he whispers. "Are you...?"

"I haven't been to a doctor yet. But yes. We're having a baby."

"Holy shit. A baby? Are you sure?" he asks as he stares at the test.

I start to panic a little, maybe he doesn't want this yet? We haven't talked about babies yet. What if he isn't ready for this? I feel a tear slip down my cheek.

"Why are you crying, baby?" He frowns.

"Are you okay with this? I swear I didn't do this on purpose."

"Mira, I can't even express how happy I am. You're going to be my wife and we're having a baby. There's nothing in this world that could make me any happier."

I reach up on my tiptoes and kiss him.

"I love you so much." He smiles as he kisses me again.

Dark Reign Session 2

Ready for the next book in the Dark Reign Session 2 series?

Caged Beauty by A. Glass

mybook.to/cagedbeauty

DARK REIGN SESSION 2 SERIES

You've felt the power that the men of Dark Reign

hold. Now it's time to fall under their rule again with new men who hold their world in their hands as they find the women who make them fall to their knees.

Power comes at a cost and these men have sacrificed their souls. They know violence, death, and how to walk in the gray, but that doesn't mean they are without weakness. The women they love are their light and they would scorch the Earth to protect them.

This December meet the men who rule their empires of crime and the women who stand by them while darkness reigns.

Check out the series and pre-order your copies today!
mybook.to/DarkReignSession2

Her Twisted Beasts by Penelope Wylde mybook.to/hertwistedbeasts
Betrayal and Ruin by Ember Davis mybook.to/BetrayalandRuin
A Delicate Omission by Layne Daniels mybook.to/ADelicateOmission

Cardinal Sin by Stormi Wilde mybook.to/cardinalsin
The Sweetest Agony by KL Donn mybook.to/TheSweetestAgony
Drawing Dead by E.M. Shue mybook.to/DrawingDead-EMS
Devil's Praise by Alana Winters mybook.to/DevilsPraise
Love in Fear by Andi Lynn mybook.to/LoveinFear
Finding My Home by Natalie Arthur mybook.to/FindingMyHome
Caged Beauty by A. Glass mybook.to/cagedbeauty
Don's Bride by S.J. Ransom mybook.to/DonsBride

About the Author

Hi! I'm Natalie. I published my first book, Aftermath in August 2021. I've been lucky enough to find my own insta-love-at-first-sight person. We have a daughter who drives us crazy and a corgi who adds to the chaos. I love hockey (Chicago Blackhawks), MotoGP (Motorcycle Racing), and baseball (Chicago Cubs). When I'm not writing, you can find me studying or crafting. Or crafting when I should be studying.

Nataliearthurbooks.com

<u>Giovanna</u>

Everything I thought about my life was a lie and because of that, trust became non-existent for me. Then I met Declan. He pushed his way into my life, determined to prove to me that not everyone is a liar. He's a hockey player and we all know the reputation of hockey players. But I want to trust someone again...maybe he's the one?

<u>Declan</u>

Hockey has been my focus for as long as I can remember. The day I met Giovanna, my life changed. Hockey would always be my first love. But she would be my last. Something happened to her and she's afraid to trust me. But that's okay, I'll show her that I'm real. That we're real.

Aftermath is the first book in my Mancini Legacy Series. All books are standalone, but it's best if read in order. There is mention of characters from my Cimaruta MC Chicago Series.

https://books2read.com/Aftermath-ManciniLegacy

Sebastiano

I had given up on meeting my person, content to be the protector of my family. Then one day I met her. But someone else was laying claim to her. If she was happy, I would step back and watch her from afar. But then I saw the marks on her and I knew I needed to save her.

Schuyler

It seems like I've been struggling most of my life. Just my

sister and me against the world. Then I thought I met the man of my dreams. Turns out he's the man from my nightmares. I can't run and I can't escape from him. Then I met Sebastiano. He made me feel safe from the moment he took my hand in his. He says I will be his, but he doesn't know about the monster that's in my life. The one that won't let go.

Saving Her is the second book in my Mancini Legacy Series. All books are standalone, but it's best if read in order. There is mention of characters from my Cimaruta MC Chicago Series.

https://books2read.com/SavingHer-ManciniLegacy

Luciana

Women on an MC council? It's unheard of until now. Love at first sight? That's a new one for me too. I was convinced I didn't need someone to make me happy.

Then I slammed into Rónán.

Literally.

In an instant, he turned my world upside down. But can he handle the MC life?

<u>**Rónán**</u>

My life was going the way I planned it. Then the most beautiful woman stepped into my path and changed my life forever. I know she's keeping things from me. And that's okay...for now.

Because she's mine.

She just doesn't know it yet.

Choices is the first book in my Cimaruta MC Chicago Series. All books are standalone, but it's best if read in order. There is mention of characters from my Mancini Legacy Series.

https://books2read.com/Choices-CimarutaMCChicago

Francesco

I met the love of my life at fourteen. She had my heart the moment I saw her. But when you're young and stupid you don't always make the right decisions. That's what happened to me. I let the temptations of my job distract me from the one thing I couldn't live without. I had lost all hope, but fate gave me another chance. I have to make it up to her. I know she's hiding something from me. Will she let me in and give me a second chance?

<u>**Maeve**</u>

I thought I had it all. Sure I may have been young, but when it's real, you just know. That was, until he ended things. I never saw it coming. Now he's back and he wants another chance. Can I really trust him not to break my heart again? I want to believe him. I've never stopped loving him. But it's not just me I have to protect anymore.

Can they find their way back to the happily ever after they were meant to have? Or will they be pulled apart again, shattering all hope?

Reclaiming Our Forever is the second book in my Cimaruta MC Chicago Series. All books are standalone, but it's best if read in order. There is mention of characters from my Mancini Legacy Series.

https://books2read.com/ReclaimingOurForever-CimarutaMCChicago

<u>Amante</u>

Relationship? No.

Love? Hell no.

Forever? Never.

A quick hook up and that was that. I had my family and my club and that's all I needed. Until the day she walked in. With her I wanted more than one night, but when I

got out of the shower she was gone. But I will find her.
Then I'll just have to convince her we belong together.

<u>Charmaine</u>

Love is nothing but a lie. I watched my parents crash and
burn and nothing and no one could change my mind.
Until him. My tattooed, hunky biker man. Wait, did I say
mine? That can't happen. But he says all the right things,
and makes me feel like I'm the most special girl in the
world. Can we make it work?

**Notch the Plan is part of the Notchin' Boots
Series. There is mention of characters from
my Mancini Legacy Series and my Cimaruta
MC Chicago Series.**

https://books2read.com/NotchThePlan-NotchinBoots

<u>Hollis</u>

The people you're born to don't always turn out to be your 'family'. Families can be chosen, and I chose the Cimaruta MC. They've been there with me for the last six years, and I thought I had everything I needed. One night was all it took to make me want more. But she's hiding something from me and I need to know what it is. I will save her from anything. That much I do know.

<u>Lila</u>

My life was finally going smoothly. It was me and my daughter against the world. I worked at a club called Club Curve—I'm a curvy girl, so why not? Then one night, HE walked in. Now he's turning my life upside down and I'm not sure how to feel about it. My biggest fear is about to become a reality.

Just as you are is a stand alone and part of the Club Curve series. But there is mention of characters from my Mancini Legacy and Cimaruta MC Chicago series.

https://books2read.com/JustAsYouAre-ClubCurve

Kostas

Mating matches keep the peace in our world. So why did it feel like my life was over when it was my turn? She hated me from the moment we were paired. And to be honest? I hated her too. So when she rejected me for some loser from another clan, it didn't bother me that much. But then I met her—the one the fates chose for me—and everything just felt right. I knew in an instant that she was the one I would never let go of.

Artemis

In our world, mates can be either fated or chosen, but finding your fated mate is never guaranteed. I thought I had chosen someone who could love me and we would spend our lives together. But then he rejected me—for my BEST FRIEND. That day, I decided I was fine being alone. But then, completely by chance, I met someone who felt like home. Could this really be it? The forever I secretly craved...my fated one.

My Fated One is part of the Fated Mates Series. There is mention of characters from my Mancini Legacy Series and my Cimaruta MC Chicago Series.

https://books2read.com/MyFatedOne-FatedMates

Aiden

Motorcycle racing has been my life since I could walk and talk. It was all I ever needed. Or so I thought. Then I met the one woman that made me want more. One day, the unthinkable happens—a racing accident causes me to lose all my memories of her. But I still feel her in my soul, even if my brain can't remember her.

Élodie

I wanted a knight in shining armor, but what I got was a wolf in disguise. After escaping from him, I met a man willing to give me everything I ever wanted. Then in a split second, he was taken from me. Not physically, but mentally. The man I love doesn't remember who I am, but I'm determined to get him back.

Racing Back to Love is part of the Forget-Me-Not Series. There is mention of characters from my Mancini Legacy Series.

https://books2read.com/RacingBackToLove-ForgetMeNot

www.ingramcontent.com/pod-product-compliance
Lightning Source LLC
Chambersburg PA
CBHW061531310726

48972CB00008B/2402